SECRET LIVES OF
CHANDLER'S FORD

Edited by Catherine Griffin

Stories written by:
Maggie Farran,
Catherine Griffin,
Sally Howard,
Karen Stephen.

Cover design: Emily Howard
Photography: John Farran

The stories in this collection reference real locations in Chandler's Ford. However, all characters and events are entirely fictional. Chandler's Ford has not yet been invaded by zombies.

Contents

Zombie Experience, Part 1   1

The Lakes   7

Peacock Blues   13

The Good Life   19

I'm More of a Bingley Girl   25

The Phone Box   31

The Yuletide Ball   37

Costa Coffee   45

If the Shoe Fits   53

Tug of Love   57

Charity Begins At Home   71

The Chalvington Road Coven   77

New Beginnings   85

Zombie Experience, Part 2   91

Afterword   109

Zombie Experience, Part 1

Sally Howard

The dead have risen to feast on the unsuspecting living. The few remaining freedom fighters are mankind's last hope. Are you ready to join them?

Sean pushed the black and red voucher, round which he'd folded a yellow Post-It note, through the letter-box of Amelie's home in Valley Park. He heard it flutter to the mat inside. He pushed the letter-box flap back into place; it was always sticking open. Harsh sunlight flashed off the shiny gold metal. He screwed up his eyes.

Goddamn headache. Hangover, more like.

He fingered his temple, trying to contain the ache. It didn't help. Not any more than the useless Paracetamol he'd taken earlier. Retrieving his aviator sunglasses from his rucksack, he parked them on his nose. They provided a smidgen of relief.

He walked down the paved drive, past well-tended beds of yellow and pink Sweet Williams. The lawn was brown round the edges, a victim of the unusually glorious summer holidays.

Amelie's mum's car was not in the driveway. Probably afternoon shopping in West Quay, with Amelie's BFF, Robyn. He smiled. Amelie would return to find the voucher for her Zombie Experience, which he had promised her. A ticket for her and Robyn for tonight's 7pm event. Saturday evenings were always something special.

Wear loose clothing, your Walking Dead T-shirt would be good, he'd written. She'd look stunning, the oversized t-shirt falling off her creamy white shoulder. And a smile playing on her cute cherry lips. After he'd chased her down sinister dark corridors, and knowing those camera blind spots, if he played his cards right, her tour would involve a little interaction with actors. An encounter of the kissing variety.

Yeah, he whistled. Or tried to. His lips were too dry, his mouth a sun-bleached sandpit. He slumped against the shelter as he waited for his bus.

Dress up as a zombie. Chase terrified participants. What could be more cool than that? His older sister had got him the dream job. He wasn't into the whole Zombie Goth thing as much as her. He and Amelie liked a laugh at the Walking Dead, that was all. His sister was well into it and had gotten a job working the late-night special shift. Come to think of it, he hadn't seen her in a while. He must text her, find out how it was going.

The bus shuddered to a halt in front of him, the doors hissing open in a fug of stale air. He stepped on the bus, rattled his change into the machine, staggered down the aisle and flopped into a seat before his knees buckled. He pressed his face against the cool glass as the green leafy trees of Valley Park slipped past his window.

The guys he worked with were great but, did they like to

2

party? Post-session adrenaline rush. And what were they drinking? A stinking sludge-coloured brew that tasted like old coins left in the hot sun, with a twist of lime.

'You know you want more,' said Carl, his luminous red-rimmed eyes flashing in the dark.

'Feed those muscles,' laughed Bevvie, squeezing his biceps. Her messed-up black hair half-hid black-painted eye sockets in a pasty white face. Boy, those make-up girls were good.

After Carl had plied him with several glasses, he'd given up being disgusted and started to enjoy it. He couldn't remember what had happened, until he woke up this morning with an almighty head.

The bus trundled on, pulling up at the abandoned Victorian hospital. The three-storey red-brick facade, with boarded-up sash-windows, was gloomy even in full sunshine. What was it like for the after-dark late-night session? He shuddered. Hurrying round the back to a modern steel door set in the crumbling wall, he punched his code into the keypad.

It was blessedly dark and cool inside. He headed to the staff room, which smelt of stale smoke and disinfectant. Carl lounged on the orange rayon sofa, tapping out a rhythm on his black tattered trousers.

'Yo, dude, rough brew last night?'

'Yeah, need a drink.'

Sean pulled a bottle from the fridge under the counter. He poured ice-cold water down his throat, feeling a deep chill as it spread through his intestines. As he tossed the bottle into the trash can, he glanced at his reflection in the mirror above the sink. 'God', he muttered, wiping the beads of sweat from his forehead with the back of his hand. His skin had a greenish-grey hue. He shivered.

3

Was this more than a hangover? The flu, perhaps? He was going straight home after his shift, to bed.

Bevvie, Jimbo and Ester came in. They were already in costume. Ester's arms were outstretched and she dragged a dead foot behind her. 'Arrgh,' she groaned.

Jimbo, her boyfriend, tall and missing an arm (it was strapped to his side beneath his clothes), threw a scrappy brown cushion at her. 'We ain't started yet, dumb skull.'

'Shut it, Jimbo.' She grinned. 'That's why I'm so good and you're a duff ball.'

Frank, their team leader, came in and clapped his hands for quiet. 'Ok, team, you're up in five. Remember the rules, everyone. Light contact only. We want to scare our guests, but not too much. And that means you, Carl.'

Carl held up his hands in a 'Who, me?' gesture.

Frank glanced to Sean leaning against the counter. 'And you, Sean, into costume, fast.'

Sean breathed hard as he waited for the starting siren. He could hardly concentrate on the screens above, which showed scratchy black and white images of the new group of innocent victims cautiously spreading their way through the dark hospital rooms. He normally loved this part of the proceedings, the thrill of the upcoming chase, the first screams echoing through the high-ceilinged rooms. His head thumped more than ever. He couldn't help gulping like a stranded fish craving air. Or something.

Through his tunnel vision, he zeroed in on one human, one with bilious meaty arms, who had stepped into his room. Three, two, one ... the siren blared. The metal starter doors swung open with a hiss. He ran, a smell like raw minced beef filling his

4

nostrils. He groaned. A real groan, not fake. As he pushed the woman into a blind corner, she laugh-cried. Saliva dripped from his mouth. Pooled on her arm. He licked it. He had an overwhelming urge to bite her. As he closed his eyes and sank to his knees, as joyous warm blood slathered down his throat, the last thought to cross his mind was of a creamy white shoulder and cute cherry lips.

Why it was important to remember that?

The Lakes

Maggie Farran

Kate hardly knew Chandler's Ford. She missed her London life. It had seemed a good idea to move out of London to leafy Chandler's Ford when she was pregnant. She and Dan had discussed the move endlessly. He was keen for his child to have a big garden and a slower pace of life.

'We'll be near the New Forest and the seaside. Chandler's Ford is a lovely place with beautiful trees. It's got a country feel and the schools are excellent.'

In the end, Dan had persuaded her to move from her beloved London, her family and friends.

Baby Alice was six weeks old now. She screamed most of the time. Kate had never felt so lonely. She hated Chandler's Ford. She couldn't care less about beautiful trees or good schools. She wanted her old life back. She felt so guilty. She had a beautiful, healthy baby and a supportive husband.

Her mobile rang.

'Hi Kate, how's it going? Are the nights any better?'

'Hi Mum. No, she seems to be waking every hour or so. I'm just so exhausted all the time. Dan is really good but he's at work now.'

Her mother had stayed with her for a week after Dan went back to work. She'd been marvellous. Now she was back in her own home in London. She had her job in the doctor's surgery to get back to.

'Why don't you put her in the pram and take her for a long walk? It will make you both feel better. Take her to the Lakes. Water always calms you down.'

Kate obediently did as her mum suggested and placed the screaming Alice into her beautiful pram. She walked towards the Lakes and Alice fell asleep. Kate felt her shoulders relax and started to look round her at the gardens. It was a warm spring day and almost every garden had a display of cheerful yellow daffodils. She reached the Lakes and carefully put the brake on the pram. She took a peek at Alice who was still sweetly asleep.

She sat on a bench and looked out over the lake. It was large and surrounded by trees which were softly reflected in the lake. The calm water glistened in the sunlight, only disturbed by the ripples made by the ducks.

A woman came towards her holding a little girl's hand. The whole scene looked like something from a Boden catalogue. The mother was smiling and the little girl was chatting away animatedly. They looked so contented. The girl started to throw bread at the ducks. The ducks didn't seem very interested.

'Never mind, Daisy, maybe the ducks aren't very hungry today. Come and sit on the bench and you can eat your snack.'

The perfect pair walked over to Kate. She stiffened.

'Do you mind if we share your bench?'

'Yes, that's fine,' said Kate. She moved along to the end of the bench as near to the pram as she could get.

The little girl started to put her raisins in her mouth carefully, one by one.

'Can I have a peek at your baby? I'm Beth by the way and this is Daisy.'

Kate pulled back the blanket and Beth looked down at little Alice.

'Oh, she's gorgeous and sleeping so peacefully. How old is she?'

'She's six weeks, but she's not usually like this. She cries most of the time. At least it seems like that at the moment.'

'It's hard at first. Daisy was like that, but it's so much easier now she can talk. At least now she can tell me why she's upset. It does get better as time goes on. No one really tells you how hard it is at first, do they?'

Kate was just about to reply when there was a loud splash. Daisy had got down from the bench and was throwing stones into the water. She stood precariously near the edge of the murky lake. Beth leapt to her feet, grabbed Daisy's arm, and shouted in fear.

'Daisy come here, you little monster. You nearly fell in.'

Daisy started to cry and flung herself on the ground in a temper, kicking her feet as her screaming got louder. Kate watched the whole scene in amazement. So life wasn't so perfect after all for Beth and Daisy. Their Boden lifestyle didn't exist.

Eventually Daisy quietened down and cuddled up to her mother. She soon looked as angelic as ever.

'Sorry about that. I don't usually shout, but to be honest I was scared stiff. Another little step and she would have been in the water. I felt guilty for not watching her properly.'

'It all happened so quickly. Don't blame yourself too much. At least Alice can't get out of her pram yet.'

Beth smiled and stroked the top of Daisy's head.

'Are you member of the National Childbirth Trust or anything like that?'

'I'm not really one of those people who join things like that. I've always made my friends through university or work.' Kate hoped she didn't sound too standoffish, but the thought of talking to other new mums about breast feeding and nappies just didn't appeal to her.

They chatted for a while and Kate found herself relaxing into the conversation and actually enjoying talking about babies and toddlers. Alice woke up and started to scream with that piercing cry that only a tiny baby knows how to make. Kate took her out of the pram and started to jig her about but she carried on crying.

'I'll have to take her home. She must be really hungry after that long sleep.'

'Why don't you feed her here? I don't mind if you don't. I used to breastfeed Daisy on this very bench. It's quiet here during the day when the children are at school. I used to find it relaxing looking at the lake. It's such a beautiful place. We're lucky to have the Lakes so near.'

Kate felt strange at first, but Beth was so easy to talk to that it all seemed quite natural. Baby Alice finished feeding and gazed up at Kate. She gave a little gummy smile.

'Wow, she smiled at me. That's her first proper smile. She must like it here.'

'Of course she does. You'll get to like it too. Just give yourself time. You've had a lot of changes in a very short time , what with leaving London and having a new baby to look after twenty four hours a day. There's a group of us that meet up on a Friday morning at that coffee shop in Hiltingbury Road. We're a friendly crowd and we do talk about other things besides babies... well, sometimes.' Beth laughed. 'Why don't you come along? Give us a chance, Kate. We might not be like your London friends but we're friendly enough.'

Kate smiled. 'Thanks, Beth. I will come along. You must think I'm terrible, going on about London all the time. I'm going to give Chandler's Ford a chance. '

She waved at Kate and little Daisy as she pushed the pram along the path. She looked into the pram and baby Alice gave her another fantastic smile.

Peacock Blues

Catherine Griffin

'Aw - awk!'

Alice jerked awake in the grey light of dawn with the certain knowledge that someone was being murdered in the garden. She grabbed Bob's arm.

'Wake up.'

He snuffled, turning away. Heart pounding, she shook him hard.

'Bob, I heard a scream. Someone's in the garden.'

'S'a bird,' he said, without opening his eyes.

A bird? Perhaps it had been more an animal sort of screech than a scream. Memory of the sound was already slipping away, and with it, her imagined conversation with a good-looking police detective.

She lay down. Green numbers gleamed on the alarm clock: 4:49 am.

'There's a peacock in the garden.' Alice turned from the

kitchen window to see her husband grabbing his sandwiches, coat half on.

'Yes, dear. See you later.'

'Why is there a peacock in the garden?' she asked his departing back. The front door slammed.

The peacock circled the bird table, pecking at the peanut fragments discarded by the blue tits. Its extravagant tail swept the close-trimmed grass. Alice glared at it from the safety of the kitchen.

When Bob returned in the afternoon, she pounced on him.

'Ted at the animal sanctuary gave it me. He couldn't pay for the roof repair, so... It's nice, isn't it? I always wanted a peacock.'

'We can't keep a peacock in the garden.'

The pocket-handkerchief patch of grass wasn't the place for a large bird. How could Bob not see that?

'He seems happy enough. I think I'll call him Howard.'

She stared at him, speechless. He began unloading the dishwasher.

'Aw – awk!'

Alice lay staring at the ceiling. From the light peeking through the curtains, she knew it was near dawn without looking at the clock. Beside her, Bob snored. He had always been a heavy sleeper. Two children, and he'd never woken once.

'Aw – awk!'

She put the pillow over her head. It didn't help much.

After breakfast, she ventured into the back garden to hang the laundry. Howard remained aloof, examining her with his evil little eyes.

'Isn't he beautiful?' The new neighbour's head appeared over the fence.

'I hope you don't mind the noise.' Alice tried to remember the woman's name. Irene? Iris?

'Oh, no. Reminds me of the Hindu Kush. I'm always up early for yoga, anyway.'

Alice pinned up the last shirt savagely.

As she went about her chores, each glimpse of Howard's snaky head and shimmying tail nudged her irritation towards anger. How could Bob do this to her? She'd made it quite clear she didn't want pets. A cat, she could maybe have lived with. Even a dog, if it was small and well-behaved.

Clutching a tea towel for defence, she slipped out of the back door and went to the side gate. She undid the bolt, pushing the gate open. The narrow path down the side of the house led from the back garden to the concrete drive and the whole wide world beyond, or at least Parkway Gardens. And from there, if it managed to cross the main road, it was only a short walk to some nice woodlands, probably ideal for peacocks.

She flipped the tea towel at Howard.

'Shoo. Stupid bird. Why don't you fly off back to the Hindu Kush?'

Howard circled the garden majestically, looking down his beak at her feeble efforts. He began pecking the nasturtiums.

She watched him through the kitchen window, seething over a lukewarm cup of tea. The idiot bird showed no inclination to escape. Patience exhausted, she took the crust from the loaf and laid a careful trail of breadcrumbs from the bird table to the open gate.

A sense of triumph flooded her as she stood, hands on

hips, watching Howard strut back and forth. Surely now he'd get the message? She decided it might be better to leave him to it, and went to have a bath.

Soaking in the hot water, she smiled to herself, anticipating the tragic scene. 'Oh no! How could the gate have been left open? The poor thing could be on the main road by now, or anywhere...'

The front door slammed.

'Alice? I'm back.' Bob's yell was pitched to carry across a construction site. He stuck his head round the bathroom door. 'Did you leave the gate open?'

'What?' She pantomimed surprise. 'Howard hasn't escaped, has he?'

'No, he's fine. You shouldn't leave the gate open, though. He could get hurt if he wanders off.'

Alice stewed in the cooling bath, bubbles bursting all around.

'Aw – awk!'

4:50am. It was no good. She steeled herself to confront Bob over breakfast.

'Darling. Howard has to go. I can't live like this.'

He chewed his toast thoroughly.

'If that's what you want, dear. I'll talk to Ted, see if we can find another home for him.'

Outside, Howard spread his glorious tail, displaying to his reflection in the French windows. Alice spread butter on her toast with a beatific sense of accomplishment. She hated to disappoint Bob, but felt she could live with it on this occasion.

Still floating on joy, she kissed her husband on the forehead and went to get the car out for the weekly shop.

16

She didn't feel anything as she reversed the Landrover. Not a bump. But she saw it in Bob's face as he came through the front door. The shout frozen unvoiced, already too late.

'What?' She looked around wildly. He opened the car door for her.

'He must have hopped over the gate,' he said. 'It wasn't your fault.'

From under the back wheels of the car, the extravagant tail spread across the drive. The morning breeze ruffled the metallic blue feathers on Howard's head and neck, lying slack on the grey concrete. Bob went to get the spade, wiping his eyes manfully.

4:48am. Alice lies awake while Bob snores in the sound sleep of the innocent. Blue tits and thrushes greet the dawn, but no sudden screeches disturb the peace of Parkway Gardens. She stares at the ceiling with hot, dry eyes. There is an old stain that looks like Austria. Or more like a strutting peacock, if you squint. She rolls onto her side and puts the pillow over her head. It doesn't help much.

The Good Life

Karen Stephen

Sheila stared out the large window to her Hiltingbury garden. *"South facing garden with a modern layout and view of the lake,"* the estate agent's blurb had read. Nigel had been thrilled.

'Just think of the parties we can have outside. Much better than this grubby little spot.' He had gestured to their cramped London yard. Gulping, Sheila had looked at the tiny patio, the old wooden furniture. The pots were bursting into life with spring flowers. It was hers. It was home.

'Just think about our lovely five bed house in Chandlers Ford. It's time we moved out of the smoke'.

'It's so far away from our friends, from the city.'

'It's on the M3. There's a mainline station with trains to London only taking seventy minutes…' He droned on, sounding like a property expert. Sheila knew the fight was lost.

Now, a few months later, they were in Chandler's Ford. Their street was leafy, their neighbours cordial. In the morning, blackbirds twittered their dawn welcome. When she opened the bi-fold doors onto their paved terrace, the air she breathed was clean and fresh. There was no background wail of sirens, no roar of traffic. He'd had a point, she conceded, ignoring the screeching peacock that shattered the tranquillity.

A cloud crossed the sun. Sheila caught a glimpse of her reflection. Her fading blonde hair looked straggly, her eyes sunken and worried. She was a dumpy 50-something housewife who'd given up on life.

She thought back to last weekend's barbecue.

'Just the partners and their wives,' Nigel had said. She'd spent all Saturday chopping vegetables for salads and slaw, creating delicious creamy dips and gooey bulging chocolate cakes. Nigel had done his man-thing, harrumphing around with pieces of charcoal. Almost setting fire to the pergola when he'd insisted on lighting the barbecue six hours before the party started.

"The partners" were florid, middle-aged men, just like Nigel. Flushed with self-satisfied success, they'd oozed around the garden drinking Pimms and champagne, sprinkling bonhomie as they went.

She had been nervous, but excited to meet "the wives". Perhaps she would find a new friend. Someone who liked crafts, the theatre, and cooking. Someone she could meet for coffee and treats at the patisserie she had noticed on Hiltingbury Road.

When the guests started to arrive, she wondered at first why so many of the men had brought their daughters. Long-limbed, caramel-haired, tawny-tanned creatures. They slunk around the men like nuzzling cats. These were second wives, or in some cases, third wives. Trophy wives.

She watched Nigel laughing and joking with the men, staring in unabashed admiration at the women. She picked at her frumpy M&S outfit, wondering if she would ever fit in.

At breakfast the next morning, Nigel said 'Why don't we join The Spa Club? Most of our new friends are members there. It's got great facilities.'

'Well, I…' Sheila felt dread flood her. She couldn't go to a Spa Club to parade around in the next-to-nothing beside these girl-women.

'It would do you good. You're carrying a bit of timber, old girl. Maybe shift a few pounds off you.'

'OK, Nigel. I get your point, loud and clear.' He regarded her over his coffee cup, eyes assessing, unwavering.

From the internet that morning, she ordered what she hoped was age and size appropriate gym gear. When it arrived, she surprised herself by liking the pastel-hued tops and black sweatpants that moulded to her limbs.

After waving goodbye to Nigel each morning, she pulled on her garb, heading off to explore Chandler's Ford. To begin with, she puffed her way around the neighbourhood streets. As the weeks passed, she ventured further from home. She greeted her walk each morning with a sense of adventure. As she strode up the wide streets, she felt a growing happiness. The gentle breeze wafted her hair, the sun warmed her face.

'Morning,' she called to the friendly-looking lady who walked her dog every morning.

'Lovely day,' she murmured to the old man who sat on the bench at the corner taking the sun.

'Your garden is beautiful.' She passed a few moments talking to Mrs Lewis who was usually tending to her flowers.

One morning, as she was returning hot but happy after a

brisk walk, Nigel was getting into his car.

'Forgot my laptop. Good lord. What you have been doing? Your face looks like a big tomato.'

The gentle summer faded to a crisp autumn. Nigel started working later in the evenings.

'Don't make any supper for me tonight. Got a meeting.'

'Who is she this time?' she muttered under her breath.

'What did you say?'

'Nothing, my pet.'

The opening bars of "Goldfinger" blasted into the quiet of the kitchen.

'Must take this call. Important business.'

He barged past her en route to the study, knocking a pile of recycling off the table.

'I've just spent twenty minutes sorting that…' He had already gone.

Sighing, Sheila massaged her forehead. Glancing towards the garden, in the fading daylight, she caught a glimpse of a woman in the window. She looked like a stranger. Sheila noticed that this woman raised her hand to her mouth at the same time as she did.

She drew nearer to her glimmering reflection. Marvelled at the disappearance of the lumps and bumps. Staring back at her was a svelte woman with toned limbs, a look of defiant confidence blazing in her eyes.

'What are you looking at?' Nigel had sneaked up behind her.

'Nothing much.'

'Darling…' His voice had the wheedling tone that signified he wanted something. 'I was thinking it would be a good idea to organise a little drinkiepops for the partners and wives before Christmas. Something festive. Invite the office staff too. Could you prepare some of your delicious food?'

A few weeks later, as the Christmas tree twinkled in the hall, Sheila smoothed her sparkly dress as she made small talk again with the partners. She felt a firm hand grab her waist.

'Mistletoe kiss!' The leering face of her husband's boss loomed towards her. 'I say, Nigel, old chap. You've got yourself a marvel here!'

Nigel, watchful as ever, raised his glass in a rueful toast.

I'm More of a Bingley Girl

Maggie Farran

It is a truth universally acknowledged, that being a rival to a boy you like doesn't help you win him. The problem really started when Miss Conway said,   'We're having a competition this term. I want you to write a short story in the style of Jane Austen. It should be about two thousand words. The winner will have their story published in the school magazine.'

Some kids groaned, but I felt really excited. I wanted to win. I looked over at Josh and we smiled, but I knew he wanted to win just as much as me.

I go to Thornden School in Chandler's Ford. It's a good school and there are lots of other kids as competitive as me. Josh has only been in my class for a month. He moved down here from the north. I liked him on that first day when our class tutor introduced him to us. He smiled and looked confident but not full of himself like some boys. He has dark wavy hair and is quite good looking, but not drop-dead gorgeous. He's in my league. I've got some hope, if you know what I mean. You have to be realistic. I'm pretty, but I don't look like a model. I know that sounds superficial. It's not all about looks. I like him as a person. He's kind and funny. He's really brainy too. He likes English like me.

We've got a brilliant teacher for English, Miss Conway. We all like her. She wears really cool clothes. She says such interesting things about the books we are studying. She listens carefully when we give our opinions and never makes us feel stupid like some teachers. I say quite a lot in her class and so does Josh. I hope it doesn't sound like boasting when I say that Josh and I are the best at English in our year.

At the moment we are studying 'Pride and Prejudice'. I expect you think I'm a bit strange, but I love it. I've seen the film where Keira Knightley plays Elizabeth. It made it easier to follow the book at first, but now I much prefer the book. I know it sounds boring but I'm more like Jane than Elizabeth. I'm not outspoken or someone with strong views. I want someone to like me straight away and stick by me. I wouldn't have given Darcy the time of day. I'm more of a Bingley girl.

After the class Josh came over and looked straight at me.

'Good luck, Maisie. You're brilliant at writing stories, but I'm not going to let you win easily.'

'You're not bad yourself. I'd say we're pretty evenly matched.' I winked. He winked back.

It all seemed friendly enough at the time, but I didn't want to be in competition with him. I liked him too much for that, but there was no way I was going to let him win. I was going to write the best story I possibly could. I went home and sat in front of my computer and waited for inspiration to strike. Nothing happened. I had a quick look on Facebook. Then I looked through my wardrobe for something decent to wear to Miranda's party on

Saturday. I was just trying on my new skinny jeans and my red top when my mobile rang.

'Hi, Maisie, it's Josh. I got your number from Miranda. I hope you don't mind me ringing you, but I just wanted to know how you were getting on with the story. Have you started it yet?'

'Hi, Josh. I'm well into it now. I've written about five hundred words. The story is just flowing out of me and onto the paper. It's like the spirit of Jane Austen is guiding me.'

I lied. I don't know what got into me. Whatever possessed me to say that to Josh? I don't understand myself. The only explanation I have is that I was desperately trying to impress him.

Anyway, we had a brief little chat, then he rang off after I told him I was keen to get back to my story before I lost my inspiration.

I was just getting started when mum fussed into my room. She pretended she was bringing me a cup of tea. I knew she was just being nosey.

'Who was that you were talking to on the phone? Was it your new boyfriend?'

'No, Mum, it's just someone from school. We were just talking about our homework.'

Mum looked disappointed. She's obsessed with me getting a boyfriend. She's always reading those romantic novels. I think it's to compensate for my dad. He must be the most unromantic man in the world although I love him to bits. Dad is one of those men who spend half their lives potting plants in the greenhouse and the other half reading car magazines.

In English the next day, Miss Conway asked us how we were getting on with our stories and I found myself lying to her too. I felt terrible when she gave me her lovely encouraging smile.

'Well done, Maisie, I felt certain you would enjoy this challenge.'

On Saturday, I went to Miranda's party. She is fourteen although she looks about seventeen. She is very pretty with a slim figure. She wears loads of eye make-up.

I didn't wear the jeans and red top in the end. I must have tried on at least five outfits. I ended up wearing my new dress from River Island. Josh was there looking fit in a black T-shirt and jeans. He smiled but we didn't get much of a chance to talk. He was too busy talking to Miranda and her best friend, Chloe. I tried not to look over in their direction too much. When I glanced over they all looked so fabulous and sophisticated. I ended up chatting to a couple of girls from my class. I felt miserable and I'm sorry to admit it, but I felt really jealous of Miranda and Chloe. I wanted Josh to be talking to me, smiling at me and no one else.

On Sunday, after I'd done my other homework, I started my story again, determined to write loads to make up for all the lies. My mind went completely blank. I just wanted to get started on my story. I felt so much pressure that everything I thought of seemed stupid. I thought about Josh. I really liked him. I didn't want to deceive him. I rang him. My hand was shaking so much I could hardly hold the phone.

'Josh, can you come over? I need to talk to you about my story. I'm a bit stuck.'

'What? You stuck? I thought you had a direct line to Jane Austen. I'll be over in half an hour.'

When he came round I told him the truth. He was really sweet and said he hadn't been able to get started either. Mum kept bringing us cups of tea and homemade fairy cakes with pink icing.

'It's really difficult to write in someone else's style. I tell you what, Maisie, why don't we write it together. We can bounce ideas off each other. It will be easier than trying to write it on our own.'

So that's how we eventually got started on our story. We decided on our main characters and then plotted the story. It was so much easier when we planned together. Josh had some brilliant ideas. I did too, by the way. Somehow all the time I was writing the story with Josh I felt like I was inspired. The story really did flow onto the page even if I didn't really have a direct line to Miss Austen. It was fun but it wasn't easy.

If I'm honest it wasn't all sweetness and light and we did disagree too. Although Josh and I worked well together, we were both competitive. Sometimes it was difficult to cut some of my own words out and admit that Josh's were better. He found the same with me, I'm sure. We worked hard on the story every day after school. We even welcomed Mum with her constant tea and questions.

'How are you two getting on with the story? It's lovely to see two young people working so well together. Would you like another cup cake, Josh?'

I must admit Josh didn't seem to find my mum as annoying as me. In fact he seemed to enjoy all the cakes. He even answered her endless questions very politely. I feel like shouting at her a lot of the time. I didn't though because I'm quite a sweet girl most of the time.

Anyway, after two weeks we gave our completed story to Miss Conway. She was delighted that we had finished in time. I'm thrilled to say that we did win the competition. Our story was published in Thornden School magazine. The best thing though is that Josh and I are brilliant friends. We do loads of things together.

He's my Mr. Bingley. For now anyway!

The Phone Box

Karen Stephen

Peggy, 1944

The setting sun glinted in Peggy's eyes as she strode up Leigh Road. The climb to Chandler's Ford seemed endless. Though her feet throbbed after her long day's work at the aerodrome, she pushed on. The barrage balloon above Eastleigh bobbed in the dwindling light. She glanced at her wristwatch. Five minutes until she spoke to Doug. Unless he was on duty, they spoke every Tuesday at this time. She was used to huddling in the phone box, whispering of love.

At the thought of his handsome, open face, the headache that had been pinching her temples receded. She thought back to that sparkling April day when they had last met. He'd been home on leave from pilot duties. The Germans seemed to have eased their bombing of the South Coast for a few days. On that warm spring afternoon, as they picnicked by the River Itchen, it seemed as if the war was a cruel nightmare. As if days spent lolling on a tartan rug, drinking lemonade and sharing tender kisses were the wonderful reality.

Sandie, 1964

Sandie wrinkled her nose. No matter how much she washed, she couldn't get rid of the smell of flour and sugar.

'That's what comes of working at the cake factory, love,' her mum had said, as Sandie sponged herself at the sink.

'I'm supposed to be meeting Dave at the Imperial. I don't want to smell like a fondant fancy.'

'Well as long as he does fancy you, all this time you spend on him.'

As she trudged in the June drizzle towards the phone box, Sandie felt a stab of irritation. Dave's floppy mop-top hair and Paul McCartney eyes had snared her the first time she'd met him. What could she do to get her mother to accept that Dave was the one?

Sandie checked she had 4d to make the call to Dave. Every Tuesday at the same time she phoned to double-check that they were meeting later that evening. She wished that sometimes he would spend some money on her and call her at the phone box. She flicked away the thought about the times she had paid his entrance to the Imperial. She knew he wasn't perfect. But she would do anything for one of his dreamy smiles.

Chloe, 2009

Chloe prodded the on/off button. Still no reception on her mobile phone. Sweat prickled her back. She had chosen the wrong clothes for the unexpected June heat. She shook the mobile phone. She could see the tall mast on the hill beyond the M3 bridge. Why on earth couldn't she get reception a few hundred metres away from it? She had to speak to Grant before six o'clock tonight. She needed to let him know that she did love him, she would go with him to New York, they had a future together.

She darted under the bridge. Ran into barriers saying the footpath was closed. Her head whipped around, looking for an alternative route. With surprised relief, she noticed the old-fashioned, squat red phone box.

Peggy, 1944

The shrill ring from the phone box pierced Peggy's thoughts. It had to be Doug. She raced to answer it.

'Doug?'

'Hello, my love'.

'How are you? Have you been busy?'

'All the better for hearing your voice, darling. There's something big going on. You've probably noticed.'

Peggy thought about the military vehicles and equipment parked around Hiltingbury. For a few months now, access to the neighbourhood had been restricted to only a few people.

'They say the King and Churchill were there recently, dear. Very hush-hush.'

'I can't say much, Peggy. Walls have ears and all that. But it's going to be exciting.' Peggy imagined his cornflower-blue eyes twinkling with the thrill of this mission. Her heart began to thud with fear.

'Just take care of yourself, Doug. I, I…' Peggy felt her voice crack.

'Darling, be calm. I don't want to blow my own trumpet but you know I'm one of the best pilots they've got.'

A sob rose in Peggy's throat. 'I know but I can't help worrying.'

'I'll be back soon. Just think of our lovely day in April. Hold on to that until we meet again.'

The hellish shriek of the air-raid siren ripped through the June evening.

'Oh, Jerry's here. I need to find shelter. Please take care, dear.'

'I'll be here. Same time, next week, Peggy darling.'

Sandie, 1964

The phone box reeked of stale fags. Sandie entered warily, careful to prevent the dank puddle splashing her sling-backs. She laid her shoulder-bag on a dog-eared directory. She must convince mum to get a phone installed. Save her from making the weekly trip to this stinking hole.

The phone trilled. Sandie felt a surge of joy. Dave was phoning her! He must care after all.

'Hello.'

A hollow silence.

'Hello, Dave?'

A faint fluttering, flickering sigh.

'Stop messing about, Dave.'

She shook the receiver, tapping it on the shelf.

Silence.

The hair on her arms stood up. Shaking, she phoned Dave. His mother said he'd already left.

Chloe, 2009

Chloe could not remember the last time she had been in a phone box; probably to make a prank call when she was a pre-teen. A sign dangled from the door: *"Decommissioned"*. It showed a

34

date one week hence. Inside smelled musty. It was sweltering in the afternoon heat.

She scrabbled in her bag for coins, hoping she had enough, not sure how much it would cost. Picking up the receiver, she froze. What was Grant's number? She replaced the receiver while she retrieved her mobile.

The old phone rang.

Startled, she dropped her mobile. It clattered onto the damp floor.

'Hello…?'

A pulsating silence.

'Hello, anyone there?'

A resonant, breathy hush.

'This is ridiculous.'

Chloe hung up. She stooped for her mobile, realising with a throb of distress that it had flooded. She couldn't retrieve Grant's number.

Sandie, 1964

Sandie wiped away tears as she tramped home in the rain. How dare Dave treat her like this? She might smell like a Mr Kipling, but she deserved better. She wouldn't be phoning him on a Tuesday night again or paying his entry to the Imperial. Sod him. Life was for living. She was going to find fun.

Chloe, 2009

Pushing open the phone box door, Chloe heard her name being called. It was Grant. He leapt from his car. The traffic billowed behind him, irate drivers pumping their horns.

'I've been looking everywhere for you.'

'I love you. I'm coming to New York.'

He enfolded her in his arms.

Peggy, 1944

The siren caterwauled. Peggy wheeled around looking for safety. She noticed a row of terraced houses to her left. If she hurried, she might make it to an Anderson shelter.

An eerie, tearing rasp squealed above the siren. The menacing, motorised wail grew closer. The doodlebug's engine cut out. A sinister silence sucked the air from the world.

In her final seconds, Peggy wondered if Doug would call her next Tuesday.

It is reputed that Chandler's Ford did have a haunted phone box. It stood outside the original Hendy Ford showroom. It was removed after repeated instances of the phone ringing with just silence on the other end when answered.

As preparation for D-Day in June 1944, the Hiltingbury area of Chandler's Ford played host to large numbers of American and Canadian troops, vehicles, and equipment. It is believed that both King George V1 and Churchill visited the area at that time.

The Yuletide Ball

Karen Stephen

'I will not allow it!'

Lydia watched her father's shaggy grey eyebrows pucker.

'It's the Yuletide ball at Hursley Hall. All of society will be going.'

'Pah. Puritans! I've never cared for them.'

'The civil war ended years ago, Father. Good King George is on the throne. All is at peace.'

'My dear child, if you remain this naïve, you're going to lead a very tedious life.' Her father picked up his snuff box.

'I'm seventeen, Father. I attended the assemblies in Winchester this summer. I've got my own visiting cards now.' She recollected the hot evenings in the Winchester assembly rooms. The crush of excited dancers. The concerned chaperones dotted around the edges of the room.

'These sorts of people are no good, Lydia.'

She remembered the handsome young man she had met at the last assembly. His warm gaze as they danced the minuet. The elation she felt. Her chaperone, Aunt Esther, whisked her away just before midnight.

'Beware, Lydia. His family were Roundheads.'

'What does that matter?' She asked during the carriage ride home. Aunt Esther feigned sleep.

Now Father was being difficult.

'No one seems to mind about the past, Father. If only you would take part in society, you would see that.'

'How dare you speak to me like that? I forbid you from going!' Lord William De Montjohn's voice rose to a roar.

'But I. . .'

'Leave!' With a shaking finger he pointed to the door.

As she left the library, Lydia's heart was pounding. She couldn't remember Father ever being this angry. Her hand fluttered to her face. Her eyes stung.

'Are you daydreaming again, Lydia?'

'Aunt Esther. I beseech you, lift my spirits.'

'I've spent the last seventeen years trying to do that, child. Let's walk in the gardens before the season becomes too cold.'

They walked arm-in-arm towards the ha-ha. The wind twitched the distant pine trees. Beyond, Lydia could imagine the din of bustling Southampton.

She sighed.

'How can father be so cruel?'

'He doesn't mean to be. Memories are long. The years of bloodshed were hard.'

'The Cromwells no longer live at Hursley Hall. How can the new owners be blamed for the sympathies of past residents?'

'Life has been unkind to him.'

'It's unfair to hold the young to ransom for their predecessors mistakes.'

'My dear, I think your father is mostly concerned about…'

'…marriage. He's only concerned about marrying me to an eligible suitor!'

They stopped. Aunt Esther grasped Lydia's hands.

'Lydia, Chilmerdon House, all of this…' She gestured to the rolling parklands, 'Is entailed to Cousin Henry. It's not yours. You've known this all your life.'

'If Mama hadn't died giving birth to me, I might have had a brother. Then this wouldn't matter.'

'Your father would still need to ensure a good marriage for you. That would not change.'

Lydia felt a surge of irritation.

'Who is this Henry to me? Why should he have such power over my home, my life?'

'Dear Lydia. It's the way of the world. Perhaps one day things will be different and we women might be able to inherit land and titles.'

'Why are you laughing?'

'It sounds implausible. Here and now, your father needs to find you a husband.'

'How can I find a husband when he won't let me go to the ball?'

'Wait till the spring, Lydia. We can travel to Bath. I hear the assemblies there are very good. There are certain to be young men of good fortune in want of a young lady. They might be more pleasing to your father.'

Later, as the shadows fell across the room, Father, Aunt

Esther and Lydia sat in silence at dinner. Lydia pushed her venison pie around the plate.

'Father, please can we...' She was interrupted by a loud cough from her Aunt.

They glared at each other.

Her father stonily focused on mother's portrait hanging over the mantel.

Lydia wondered what life would have been like had mother lived.

A few days later, she heard a murmur of voices from the hallway. Intrigued, she crept from her room, startling a maid who was sweeping the floor. She found a hiding place behind a suit of armour.

'Sir Benedict Gillbride begs leave to attend Lord William De Montjohn.'

It was the young man from the Winchester assembly. Startled, Lydia knocked against the metal armour. The clang echoed throughout the hall. Sir Benedict glanced towards the noise.

Her cheeks burned. Please don't let him see me, she thought as she cowered behind the banister.

Gillbride laid his card on the salver presented to him by the steward. Lydia regarded his chiselled features, his fashionable winter cloak. She felt a strange, giddying sensation.

'Lord De Montjohn is not receiving visitors this morning Sir Gillbride.'

'That is regrettable. Please present him with my warmest courtesies.' The steward steered Sir Gillbride towards the door.

Gillbride paused.

'I wish to extend again an invitation to the Yuletide ball at

40

Hursley Hall to the esteemed Lord, his charming sister and daughter.' Sir Benedict raised his voice, peering towards the stairs.

The library door crashed open.

'Dashed Roundhead! Get out of my house.' Father scurried towards Sir Benedict.

'Kind Lord, I came merely to...'

'Shooh! Go! Steward, get this man of my house.'

With one final alarmed glance towards the stairs, Gillbride left.

Behind the banister, Lydia flinched.

'Aunt Esther, please beg Father to let me go to the ball. He doesn't have to attend himself.' They were walking in the gallery that afternoon.

'I fear your father's mind is set.'

Aunt Esther squeezed her arm.

As she lay in bed that night, Lydia heard raised voices from the drawing room. Her father's angry shouts. The soothing tones of Aunt Esther. The slam of doors. Her pillow grew wet as she realised Father would not relent.

She awoke on Friday to heavy hoar frost. Turbulent grey clouds scudded across a sky tinged with pink. She studied her emerald velvet gown. It would have been perfect for the ball.

She gazed at the tiny portrait of Mother which lay on the bureau. In contrast to the more formal portrait downstairs, this painter had captured mother smiling with a playful gleam in her eyes.

A tentative knock at the door.

'I erm...' Father stood hesitant, looking out of place in her room. 'Esther tells me that I'm being an old fuddy-duddy. That time moves on.'

Lydia dared not speak.

'What have you there?' She held out the miniature to him. 'Your mother was a real beauty.'

'What was she like?'

'Spirited. Lively. You remind me of her.'

'I will regret not knowing her for all of my life.'

'She would have known what do about so many things.'

Lydia watched as pain etched Father's face.

'Her parents did not want us to marry. They were Puritans, Roundheads. She never recovered her health. It was the worry, you see.'

Sadness washed over Lydia.

'As tiresome as you can be, I love you, my vivacious girl. Esther is right. You young things need to be free to make your own friendships, to go your own way.'

He glanced at her gown.

'You will be the toast of the ball, my dear.'

'I can go?'

'Against my better judgement, yes, you can. There are certain caveats.'

'Anything, father.'

His bushy eyebrows crinkled.

'The carriage will return at midnight. Don't be late!'

From the doorway, he winked.

Hursley estate passed into the Cromwell family in 1643 when Oliver Cromwell's son Richard married Dorothy Major, daughter of the owner, Richard Major. Richard Cromwell lived with his wife in Hursley from 1649 until 1658 when he was proclaimed Lord Protector following the death of his father. This made Hursley briefly the country seat of the ruler of England. It was not to last however as Richard's grip on power was weak, he was forced from office within months and by 1660 concerns for his safety forced Richard Cromwell to flee the country with Dorothy. They travelled first to France and then to other parts of Europe where Richard lived under an assumed name. Richard's son Oliver Cromwell II took over the Hursley estate. Richard returned to Hursley after Oliver died in 1705 and lived on as lord of the manor until he died in 1712 whereupon he was buried in the chancel of All Saints' Church, Hursley. Richard's daughters sold Hursley estate in 1718.

Costa Coffee

Maggie Farran

Jenny sat at a table by the window. She sipped her cappuccino as slowly as she could. She looked out of the window and sighed. It was already half past ten. He was half an hour late.

He'd looked so fit on Tinder. He'd sounded great in his e-mails. She had arranged to meet Tom at the new Costa in Chandler's Ford. She might have known it was too good to be true. She was just about to leave when she saw someone who looked just like his photo rush in and scan the coffee shop. He saw her, smiled, and walked over to her table.

'Hi, you are Jenny aren't you? I'm so sorry. What must you think of me being so late? I'm surprised you didn't give up on me. My mum had a bit of a problem with her washing machine. It was about to flood her kitchen. I had to sort it out for her.'

'Oh well, you're here now, Tom. '

'Can I get you another coffee and something to eat?'

Tom brought two cappuccinos and some crunchy oat biscuits back to the table. He sat down opposite her. There were a

45

few awkward silences at first, but soon the conversation flowed.

'I'm a teacher at Fryern Infant School. I've been there a year now. My family all live in Liverpool, but I wanted a change and so I moved down here.' Jenny tried to sound like she thought it was a good idea.

'My family all live round here. I work at Bodysound as a fitness instructor.' Tom grinned at her.

They chatted quite happily for an hour or so. Jenny felt relaxed with him. He was easy to talk to and he listened which made a change from some of her previous dates.

'I'd better go,' Tom said. 'My mum expects me for Sunday lunch. It's a bit of a ritual. She loves having her brood round her on a Sunday. To be honest, it suits me too. No-one cooks a roast like your mum, do they? I'd like to meet up again. If you want to, that is?'

'Yes, I'd like that. Text me and we'll arrange something.' Jenny tried not to sound too keen. She hadn't had much success with boyfriends in the last few months. She'd been on a few dates but nothing remotely serious.

She phoned her mum when she got home.

'How did it go, dear? What was he like? Do you think you'll see him again?' Her mum meant well but she was always full of questions.

'He was really nice, Mum. We're going to meet up later in the week, all being well.'

Once the niceties were over with, her mother launched into a blow-by-blow account of her week.

'Well that's about it love, we all miss you. When will you next be coming home?'

'I'll be home for the Christmas holidays. I miss you all too.

Bye Mum.'

Jenny put the phone down. She curled up on the cherry red sofa and gazed out of the window. She had come down south so full of hope and excitement. The truth was, none of it had turned out as she expected. She loved her job, but it just wasn't enough. A lot of the time she felt lonely. She missed her warm, lovely family like mad, but there was no way she was giving in and going back to Liverpool.

She made herself a healthy tuna sandwich. Half an hour later she ate her way through a packet of chocolate hobnobs washed down by three cups of tea. She spent the remainder of Sunday marking books and doing lesson preparation. In the evening she watched 'Downton Abbey'.

She loved the programme but it was not the same on your own. She remembered squashing up on the sofa at home with her sister and her mum. They used to make comments all the way through. That had been half the fun. She felt really sorry for herself when her mobile bleeped to tell her she'd got a text.

I really enjoyed meeting you. How about cinema Wednesday eve? The new Bond film? Tom

She tapped out a reply. *Thanks Tom that would be great. See you Wednesday. Jenny*

On Wednesday, Jenny put on her new skinny jeans and blue top. She looked in the mirror and was pleased with what she saw. Her ginger curls framed her face gently for once. She put on a bit of eye liner and mascara.

Tom picked her up punctually this time. They both enjoyed the film and went to the King Rufus for a drink afterwards.

'How are you enjoying life down south then?'

Jenny didn't know quite how to answer. She didn't want to appear negative or needy.

'I'm getting to like it. I'd like to get to know a few more people except for other teachers. I miss my family like mad.'

'Tell me about them. I love hearing about other people's families.'

'I've got one sister, Lucy. She's a couple of years younger than me. She's very bubbly. We get on really well. She still lives at home. My mum's a teacher like me and she's always been so supportive. My dad has ginger hair and the temper that goes with it. He loves his garden and grows all his own vegetables. He plays the guitar for fun, but he's pretty good. I miss them a lot, but I couldn't stay in Liverpool all my life.'

'What made you choose Chandler's Ford?'

Jenny fiddled with her hair and smoothed down a curl. 'I came down here with my boyfriend, Sam, but it didn't work out. He had a job with IBM in Hursley. He changed a lot. He got bored with me and found someone else.'

Tom looked uncomfortable. There was a long awkward silence.

'Sorry, Jenny, I didn't mean to pry. I think you're lovely anyway. '

Jenny could feel herself blushing. 'Thanks, Tom, you weren't to know. Anyway I'm over it now. He was an arrogant so-and-so. He only ever thought of himself. I'm better out of it really.'

'I know you might think this is a bit of an odd suggestion, but why don't you meet my family? I know they'd like you. Come to lunch with us all on Sunday.'

'I'd love to, but what would your mum say?'

'She's dead relaxed. The more the merrier as far as she's

48

concerned. She's ever so easy to talk to. You'll get on like a house on fire.'

After the school day had finished Jenny went to the staff room to make herself a cup of tea. Emma was there marking a huge pile of books. Emma worked in the same year group as Jenny, which had thrown them together in a rather artificial way.

Jenny smiled at Emma, 'Would you like a cup of tea? I'm just making one.'

'Yes please. I'm parched. I've had a really tiring day. Was that Tom I saw you with in The King Rufus the other day? You two looked very close.'

Jenny felt herself blushing. She hadn't noticed Emma there, but then it was quite a spacious pub with lots of different eating areas. 'Yes, we'd just been to the cinema. Do you know him?'

'He's one of the fitness instructors at Bodysound. I'm a member. All the girls like him and some of the older ladies too. He's quite a charmer. He's been out with loads of the members. He's very popular, if you know what I mean.' Emma gave a knowing wink.

At home that evening Jenny felt very uncomfortable. She really liked Tom, but she couldn't stand the thought of being hurt again. The whole episode with Sam had left her feeling fragile. Tom had seemed so kind and genuine, but Emma had made him sound like a right Casanova. She jumped as her mobile rang. It was Tom.

'Hi Jenny, are you still on for lunch on Sunday? I've got to let my mum know. She always wants to meet my girlfriends, but this is the first time I've ever wanted to take any girl home.'

'Is that what you tell all your girlfriends?'

There was a long silence. 'What do you mean, Jenny? Who

have you been talking to?' Tom sounded hurt.

'It's just something Emma at work said, about all the women at Bodysound falling at your feet.'

There was another long silence. 'Jenny, please don't believe anything Emma says about me. She's got a bit of an axe to grind. I'd forgotten she worked at the same school as you. We went out for a bit over a year ago. She seemed like a nice girl, but she just wasn't right for me. I tried to break up with her gently, but to be honest it wasn't mutual. She was really angry. She just couldn't seem to accept the relationship was over. She was always texting me. She was desperate for us to get back together. In the end I just had to cut her right out of my life. It was a horrible episode.'

Jenny felt awful. She should have trusted her own feelings and not believed Emma. 'I'm so sorry, Tom. I didn't know what to think. Yes, you can tell your mum I'd love to come to lunch on Sunday. I can't wait to meet your family.'

On Sunday, Tom picked her up and took her to his mum's house in Park Road. His mum opened the door and beamed with delight.

'You must be Jenny. I've been so looking forward to meeting you. Tom can't stop talking about you. I've never met any of his other girlfriends.'

Tom blushed scarlet and gave his mum a hug. 'Now you know why I've never brought any girl home before. Mum doesn't know the meaning of the word discreet.'

Jenny laughed. 'At least I'll know how your mum really feels. I like people to be straightforward and honest.'

'Me too,' said Tom's mum. 'I know you might think this is a funny question, but do you like Downton Abbey? It's the last episode tonight and I'm an addict.'

Jenny smiled. 'It's my favourite. Can I watch it with you this evening? I enjoy it so much more when I'm with another fan.'

Tom's mum squeezed Jenny's arm and grinned at Tom. 'I can tell we're going to get on well already.'

If the Shoe Fits

Sally Howard

I could tell it was Marcus by the shoes he wore. And I should know, I'd spent enough time staring at them. Brown patent leather, a little scuffed across the top - did he go straight from work to kick around a football, I wondered? Well-made, expensive shoes, probably from the bootmakers by the cathedral in Winchester. Appropriate to his charcoal grey suit and muted tie. Nothing wrong in that.

So why did he have to wear white socks with them?

I was pondering this question as I swung my car into the parking space under the pine trees. It was set to be a lovely day, despite being a Monday. I pulled my work bag from the passenger seat and locked the car. Monday meant he would be turning up at my desk, as he did every Monday and Wednesday to get the accounts reconciled. I badged into work and headed up the stairs to my office. Every time he came by, I'd try to see whether he was wearing his white socks. This involved a lot of bending down, staring at the ground, fiddling with the buckle on my shoes. He must think I was a right clumsy clogs, always dropping my pen or something.

Last week, I nudged a paper with my elbow. We'd both bent down together. I really thought he'd twigged what I'd done, and my cheeks were burning.

I'd even mentioned it to Janice, who worked in his area, the accounts department. She was on the case.

'Brown socks, every day except "you" days,' she reported, blowing the froth on her cappuccino. We'd taken our usual walk up the hill to Costa Coffee for our lunch hour.

'I guess he must go to gym or something after work.' I hesitated. 'There's probably a perfectly reasonable explanation.'

I put down my cup, nearly spilling the coffee: 'Er, you don't suppose, oh my, you don't suppose, he thinks I like them, do you?'

Janice bit her lip, then a smile brightened her face: 'I've an idea. Let's test it out. Next week, they're changing to Tuesdays and Thursdays to gather the account information. So if he comes to work in white socks on Tuesdays and Thursdays, we'll know.'

'Brilliant idea, Sherlock.' I knew I could rely on Janice.

Tuesday of the following week, I knew that Marcus would be coming round my desk mid-morning. I'd had plenty of time to cook up a fool-proof white-sock-spotting plan.

By eleven thirty though, when he still hadn't arrived, I was a little bit anxious. The heating in the room was on full steam despite the Spring sunshine, which sparkled on the pale green lawn outside my window.

Suddenly he was there behind me. I swung round from my abstract gazing out of the window to see him grinning, a faint flush on his cheeks too. Must be hotting up over there in accounts already, in the frantic run up to the end of the financial year.

'Hi,' he said.

'Hi,' I said.

My plan was to invite him to sit down. Easy viewing of socks would ensue. Simple. My office mate, previously briefed, obliging left the room.

'I'm sorry,' I said, 'I just need to pull up the figures. Why don't you take a seat?'

I heard the creak of the seat as he sat down next to me. I stared at the computer screen, but it could have been blank for all I saw. How could I think it wouldn't be so obvious? He had nothing to do but rock back in his seat, foot elegantly perched on his knee, and watch me! I just couldn't move my eyes in his direction. Rigid in my seat, I clicked randomly on the screen. My thick jumper had seemed like a good idea this chilly morning, but, honestly, now I was really burning up.

When I couldn't possibly pretend to click any more windows, I sent the entire document to the printer on my desk. I sat there, looking down, fiddling with my pen, as the printer chugged its way slowly through the pages.

I realised the printer was silent. Now was my last chance. I slowly raised my eyes, up from the floor, past his neat brown shoes, past his white socks and into the sparkle of his grey-flecked eyes.

'Oh,' I said.

'I only wear white socks so you'll notice me,' he said.

'Oh,' I repeated.

'I don't really like white socks, but you did seem to be quite taken with them.'

'Oh.'

'So I kept wearing them.'

He paused. 'Say something.'

Scarcely able to breathe, I said: 'I was kinda wondering ...'

So now I know Marcus by the shoes he wears, his brown patent leather, his Nike trainers, his hiking boots, those well-worn flip-flops on the beach ...

Tug of Love

Catherine Griffin

Mariah stopped before the white UPVC front door of the maisonette in Milford Gardens. Nothing had changed. Still the same street, still the same house that had been home for two years. It didn't feel like home any more.

Her finger hovered over the doorbell for a moment before she pushed it. A faint ding-dong echoed from inside. While she waited, she adjusted her smile – polite, friendly, firm -- and hooked a vagrant blonde curl behind her ear. Footsteps sounded, followed by the click of the latch.

Lee opened the door. Like the house, he looked no different than when she'd last seen him two weeks ago. Still the same chiselled cheek bones and soulful brown eyes she'd once loved. No black circles under those eyes. No sudden weight gain. Her smile tightened.

'What do you want?' he said.

'Only what's mine.'

She stepped into the hallway, forcing him either to bar her

way or allow her in. He retreated into the living room.

The coffee table, the one she'd bought from IKEA, was littered with bicycle parts, pizza boxes, and unopened junk mail. With his back to her, he picked up a couple of items and dumped them into the overflowing bin. The air smelt of unwashed socks, Indian takeaway, and unchanged cat litter.

On the sofa, a ginger lump uncurled and yawned, showing a pink tongue and white teeth. Slitted yellow eyes blinked at her sleepily. She dropped the cat carrier on the floor.

'I put your DVDs over there.' Lee pointed to a pile on the floor by the book case. 'Help yourself.'

'Thanks.' She flicked a cursory glance at the boxes. 'I'll take Loki today too.'

Lee looked at the cat carrier as if he hadn't previously noticed it, though he surely must have.

'You said your sister was allergic.'

Mariah tossed her hair back. 'She has pills. Besides, I'll get my own place soon.'

'But... this isn't what we agreed. This is his home.'

She walked over to the sofa and ran her fingers through Loki's smooth warm fur. He rolled over.

'I didn't agree to anything. He's my cat. Look, you can keep the TV, OK?'

'Just a minute.' Lee turned to her with that familiar crease between his eyebrows. 'He was never your cat. He's our cat. Jointly. I have just as much right to him as you do.'

'He is too my cat.' Sure, they'd picked him out together at the cat shelter, but it was her birthday. He'd been her birthday present. 'You never really wanted him. Why are you being so petty and selfish?'

'Me, selfish? What does that make you?'

'I'm taking him, and that's that.' She scooped the sleepy cat into her arms. His purr vibrated through her chest. 'C'mon baby. You want to come home with mummy, don't you?'

Lee moved between her and the door, spreading his arms wide. 'No.'

'What are you going to do? Hit me? You'd like that wouldn't you? Make you feel a big man.' Her arms tightened on Loki, who twisted. He never liked being squeezed.

Lee closed the distance between them in two strides, kicking the cat carrier in passing. He snatched at her wrist. She stepped back. The back of her legs hit the sofa, and she tumbled onto the cushions. Loki wriggled from her grip and scrambled away,.

'Ouch.' A scratch marked her bare forearm. 'Now look what you've done.'

Lee crossed his arms. Loki had leapt over the back of the sofa and disappeared from sight.

'Just take your DVDs and go. And the TV if you want. I don't care about any of that stuff. But you aren't taking Loki. Not today, not ever.'

She grabbed the carrier bag of DVDs and left. Defeat smarted more than the scratch on her arm. Lee didn't care about Loki like she did. He just wanted to see her miserable. Well, if he thought she was just going to give in, he was sorely mistaken.

Milford Gardens lay quiet in the cool night, lit by the glow of street lamps. Parked cars lined the street. A few houses showed lights behind drawn curtains, but most were already dark and silent, the residents having gone to bed.

Mariah checked her watch. No light showed from the maisonette. Lee was most likely asleep by now; he was a creature of habit.

She took a deep breath and got out of the car. From the passenger seat she took the cat carrier and her other supplies. All was quiet as she approached the white UPVC door with the cat flap.

Crouching by the door, she applied the can opener to a tin of tuna. The fishy smell was strong even to her nose. She put the open can on the ground, then pushed open the cat flap and peered through. Nothing moved in the hall. No yellow eyes gleamed from the darkness.

'Loki,' she crooned quietly. 'Here, puss, puss, puss.' She wafted the tuna in front of the cat-flap.

Something thumped near the wheelie bins. She span round and saw a grey shape, tail making a question mark in the air.

'Oh, Loki. You gave me a fright. Come here, baby. Pst, pst, pst.'

The cat meandered over, sniffing the air.

'That's it. Look, tuna. Nice tuna.'

As soon as the cat got within reach, she grabbed it by the scruff of the neck. It made a low yowl but didn't resist as she shoved it into the cat-carrier. The cat continued to growl, a sound that made the hair on the back of her neck stand up. She couldn't remember Loki ever making such a noise.

'Ssh. Settle down, baby. You'll be home soon.'

Wide wild eyes stared out at her.

From behind her came the sound of a cat enthusiastically tucking into a tin of tuna. She turned. The new cat looked up at her, purring. It looked familiar.

'Oh, hells.' She frowned at the cat carrier. 'You aren't Loki, are you?'

The caged cat growled.

She looked back at the new arrival. 'Loki?'

His ears twitched. Cautiously, she reached out to grab him. Loki backed away.

'C'mon Loki. Come to mama.' She wiggled her fingers in best cat-beguiling style and inched towards him. He held his ground, cocking his head on one side curiously.

She launched herself at him. Her outstretched hands clasped air as she thumped full-length onto the lawn. She picked herself up from the damp turf, spat out some grass, and looked round for the cat.

He'd climbed the rowan tree which overhung the wheelie bins, and now crouched on a spindly branch, too high for her to reach. He couldn't go any higher, and since she'd stupidly scared him, he wasn't likely to come down. How could she get to him?

She dragged the black wheelie bin under the tree. If she climbed on it, she could reach Loki. Assuming she didn't fall off first.

Loki watched with interest as she swarmed onto the bin. She sat on it. It seemed fairly stable, so she got onto her knees. She still couldn't reach Loki. He'd retreated back to the tree trunk. His eyes shone yellow from the shadows.

'All right.' She took a deep breath. 'Just stay there, I'll come and get you.' She got one foot under her, and then the next, and gingerly straightened her legs. The bin wobbled, but she was standing. She grabbed the branch Loki sat on. Though it was barely more than a twig, it was reassuring to have something to hold.

She slid her other hand along the rough bark until she encountered soft fur. Loki pushed his round head into her hand, purring like an engine. She petted him, then dug her fingers into his scruff and pulled.

Unfortunately, Loki had other ideas. He dug his claws into the branch. She pulled harder. For a few seconds, her muscles battled his grip and neither moved.

Then he let go. She had a flash of triumph as she realised she'd got him, then the world went sideways.

There was a moment of free-fall, just time enough to discover that she and the wheelie bin were moving in different directions, and her direction was going to see her on the ground very soon.

'Shit.'

Instinctively, she released the cat and tucked her head in her arms.

Soggy turf struck her hard, knocking the wind from her lungs. She lay shaking and confused, wondering how her fall could have made that loud thump of heavy plastic hitting concrete. The window nearest her glowed yellow. Her thoughts began to reassemble themselves. Luckily, she'd fallen on the grass, not the concrete. She didn't think she was injured. The wheelie bin had fallen over. And the noise had woken Lee.

She heard the front door being unlatched. In a panicked rush, she scrambled to her feet and scuttled away.

Two days passed. Mariah nursed her bruises and tried to put the memory of her adventure behind her. Regretfully, she had to admit she wasn't going to get Loki now. Maybe if she left it a month or two, Lee would have got tired of his game. He couldn't keep resenting her forever, could he?

When her phone rang and she saw the familiar number,

her heart leapt. He must have seen sense quicker than she expected.

'Hello?'

Only heavy breathing answered.

'Lee, stop messing about. What do you want?'

'You've got him, haven't you?'

'What?'

'Don't bother denying it. I found what you left behind. You've... cat-napped Loki. Well, I hope you're pleased with yourself, you devious little bitch.'

'What? No! I haven't got Loki.'

'Don't lie. Just tell me he's safe, that's all I want.'

'I don't have him. Listen, Lee. I'm telling the truth. I admit I tried to take him, but he got away. Why would I lie to you? He isn't here.'

More heaving breathing, then the call was cut off. Mariah sat with the phone in her sweating hand. If Lee thought she had Loki, then he didn't have Loki. So where was Loki?

After a sleepless night, Mariah spent most of her work day staring out of the window, worrying. If Loki had run away that night, he would most likely have gone home by now. Unless something had happened to him... But no, he did wander off sometimes, for a day or two. He'd go back to Lee before long. Not that Lee would think of letting her know, the selfish bastard. She could worry herself sick for all he cared.

On Saturday afternoon, she put on her coat and set out on foot for Milford Gardens. Walking helped her mood. It was a mild spring day, the sort of day when you can't believe anything bad could happen. She would just go to the road and see if Loki was about. If she didn't see him, she might knock on the door. Lee wouldn't be happy to see her, but she wasn't scared of him. She had a right to know if Loki was safe.

On Oakmount Road she saw the first sign. Carefully taped to a lamppost: Missing Cat, in bold letters, over a blurry photo of Loki.

It was really true then. Lee wouldn't go to this sort of trouble just to annoy her. Loki was lost, and it was her fault.

She stopped to stare at the next sign she passed, though it was identical to the first. Tears stung her eyes. Poor Loki. If only Lee had handed him over when she'd asked, this wouldn't have happened. It was as much Lee's fault as her own. More, really.

She dug among the till receipts and sweet wrappers in her handbag and excavated a biro. She scribbled out Lee's phone number on the sign, and over the top wrote her own mobile number.

There. She stepped back to admire her handiwork. It wasn't wrong. Loki was hers. Lee was going to find out she meant business.

She walked the length of Oakmount Road and the surrounding streets, changing every sign she found. By the time she had finished, she was footsore and exhausted, but glowing with satisfaction at a job well done.

The evening passed, and next day, and no one called about Loki. Neither did Lee call to shout at her. By the day after that, she began to suspect something was wrong, and went to check on the signs.

Anger choked her when she saw what he'd done. He'd stuck new signs over the ones she'd changed. Every bloody one. There were more too, hundreds of them. Every lamppost, tree, and bus stop had a sign.

It was impressive, in a way. She'd never suspected he could be so diligent. If he'd put half so much effort into applying for jobs he might not be working in a bike shop, and then...

But that line of thought wasn't helpful. Lee was happy going nowhere. She wanted more from life, and didn't mind working hard to get it.

Grimly, she uncapped a brand-new Sharpie and set to work.

Half-way up Oakmount Road, Sharpie in hand, she came face to face with Lee, going the other way with a stack of new signs under his arm. They both stopped.

'You!'

'You bitch.'

'Bastard.'

They stared at each other. Mariah couldn't think of anything further to say, but knew she wasn't going to back down, no matter what.   The stand-off could have continued for some time, if her phone hadn't rung. She ignored it for a moment, but then Lee's phone also went off.

She snatched her phone from her bag and answered.

'Hello?'

A woman's voice gabbled. Mariah grabbed a few key words from the flow.

'My cat? Did you find him?'

'What's happened?' Lee said to his own phone.

Mariah felt dizzy. She tried to listen to the rushed explanation from her caller, but as the facts sunk in the woman's stream of commiseration turned into meaningless noise.

'Where is he?' she said, and heard Lee say the same words,

a fraction out of sync.

She put her phone back in her handbag. Their eyes met again, and in his she saw mirrored her own fear.

'I'll drive,' he said.

'Are you the owners?' the vet said.

'I am,' Mariah replied, and heard Lee echo her. She glared at him.

'Uh. Right. Come this way, then.' The vet led them into a tiled, disinfectant-scented corridor. 'We need to have a little chat.'

'Can I see him?' Lee said.

The vet paused, holding open the door to his office. 'I don't think that would be a good idea. He's in a bad way, I'm afraid.'

Numbly, Mariah walked in and took a seat. 'What happened?'

Lee sat next to her, their arms touching.

'A car. His jaw and front legs are broken.' The vet held up an X-ray.

'Is he...' The words wouldn't come.

'Can you fix him?' Lee said.

The vet perched on the edge of the desk. 'That's what we have to discuss. I can operate, but I can't guarantee he'll walk again. Do you have pet insurance?'

'No.' Lee shook his head.

Mariah stared at him. 'What?

Lee ignored her. 'What will it cost?'

'Over two thousand pounds,' the vet said. 'I quite understand if you don't want to go ahead. In fact, it may be the kindest thing...'

'I'll pay,' Mariah said. She straightened in her seat. It would empty her savings account. She felt a brief pang at the thought. The money was meant for a deposit on a house, or had been, until the break-up. But Loki's life was more important.

'What?' Lee said. 'No, I'm not going to let you do this. You think you can just buy whatever you want, don't you?'

'You don't have the money, I do.'

'I can pay. I'll take a loan out.'

'Ha. Don't make me laugh.'

The vet coughed. 'I can see this could take a while to sort out. But as long as someone's prepared to pay, we'll go ahead with the operation.'

He gave both of them paperwork to sign. Mariah scrawled her name with a shaking hand.

'Why don't you two go away and sort out between yourselves how you want to finance this? It'll be several hours before there's any news. I'll call you. Both of you.'

Lee said nothing. He held the door for her on the way out, but she didn't look him in the eye. She made it as far as reception, empty of other patients since the practice was shut for the day, and collapsed into a plastic seat.

Tears came and she couldn't hold them back. She sobbed into her hands.

'You really love him, don't you?' Lee said. He'd sat down beside her.

'Of course I bloody do.' As fast as she wiped away the tears, more came. She blew her nose into a disintegrating tissue.

'I thought you were just angry with me.'

'Yes, because that's how you feel. You don't care about Loki, you just want to make me miserable. Well, you have, are you

67

happy now?'

Lee stared at the floor. 'I don't want you to be miserable. I never did. But Loki was the only good thing I had, when you left.'

They were both silent. She sniffed. A warm arm encircled her shoulders.

'He's tough. He'll be OK,' Lee said.

She leaned into his shoulder and closed her aching eyes.

She awoke to the tinny jangle of her phone ringing. Muzzy with sleep, she couldn't understand why she was curled up in a hard plastic chair with her head wedged against Lee's shoulder. Then she remembered where they were and dived for her bag.

'Hallo?' She fumbled with the phone, but had been too slow.

A second later, Lee's phone rang.

'Yes?'

She watched his face as he listened.

'Yes.'

The voice on the other end sounded like a spider in a matchbox.

'Yes.'

She squeezed Lee's arm to remind him she was waiting for news too.

'Yes.'

He closed his eyes and bowed his head as he took the phone from his ear.

'What?' She shook him. 'What's happened? Is he all right?'

'The vet says...' He covered his face with his hands. '...He says the operation went as well as it could.'

'Oh, thank God.' She threw her arms round him and

hugged him tight, just for the comfort of his solid human warmth.

'It's all right. He's going to be all right,' Lee said.

She pulled away first, to wipe away the tears of relief and blow her nose on a fresh tissue.

'I must look a mess.'

'You look fine.'

'Don't.' She composed herself. 'Let's sort this thing out. Like grown-ups, for once.'

'OK.' He straightened in his seat, his expression guarded.

She took a deep breath. 'I'll pay the vet bill.' She held up a finger to forestall his reaction. 'You can pay me back half. Interest free, in instalments'

Mental gears turned.

'And what about Loki?'

This was harder. 'You should take him. He needs familiar surroundings, at least until he's better. But...'

'But?'

'I want visitation rights.'

Silence stretched as they both watched each other.

'All right.' He nodded. 'I think we can do that. And when he's better?'

'We don't need to decide that now. Let's just see how we get on.'

Lee looked puzzled, as if he was trying to figure out the catch in the arrangement. Mariah smiled. She had a funny feeling she wouldn't need to find her own flat, after all.

Charity Begins At Home

Karen Stephen

Fat raindrops soaked Charlotte as she strode towards the Fryern bus stop. Held up at the office again, she felt frazzled and agitated. A picture of a lost cat dangled from a lamppost. Traffic sloshed through dank puddles. Waiting at the pedestrian crossing, a glint from a shop caught her eye.

She peered through the dusty windows at mannequins posing in nautical-themed clothes. The haphazard clash of styles and eras indicated it was a charity shop. Scanning the interior, she spied the source of the brightness. A shiny china box twinkled under the overhead lights. Without stopping to think, she pushed open the door.

'Can I help you, my dear?' An elderly woman behind the counter contemplated Charlotte over tortoiseshell cats-eye spectacles.

'I didn't know this shop was here.'

'We only opened today. Take a look around.'

Charlotte felt the familiar allergic tickle in her throat. Dust and mothballs. She normally avoided these shops.

'Is this what you're looking for?' A hint of Youth Dew perfume. The woman had scuttled to Charlotte's side.

Among shelves of random ornaments and mismatched cups, the box glimmered.

'Genuine Art Deco. Only £20.'

'Oh, that's too much. I couldn't. Ben, my husband...' Charlotte thought back to Ben's despair last night. 'You see our boiler has just broken down.' The assistant nodded sympathetically. 'Last month we had to replace our car. It's one thing after another.' Charlotte felt tears pool behind her eyes.

'Hold it. See how it feels.' Charlotte took the box from the assistant. About the size of a paperback, it was smooth and cool. It glowed with elegant Art Deco shades of pink and gold.

'Does it open?' Charlotte's fingers had found a switch.

'Not yet. You never know though.'

Charlotte turned it this way and that. She could imagine it on her dressing-table catching the morning light.

'It's lovely. Where did it come from?'

'Hard to say, my dear.'

'I'd love it but...no.'

The woman tapped her mouth with her painted fingernail. 'Tell you what, as it's our opening day, I'll sell you it for £5.'

Charlotte made some rapid calculations. What would Ben say? Things were tight.

'Look after it.' The assistant handed the tissue-paper wrapped box to Charlotte.

Later, as Charlotte positioned the box on her dressing-table, Ben's voice drifted upstairs.

'Honey, I'm home.'

She fluffed her hair and slicked on some lipstick. 'Good day?'

His smile didn't reach his tired eyes. 'More cutbacks are expected. I asked the boss but he wouldn't comment.'

'Oh Ben, we can barely afford the mortgage as it is. What would we do if you lost your job?'

'Run away? Sell peanuts on a beach?'

'Ben, be serious. What would we do? What about a ba…?'

'Don't worry. Everything will work out OK.' He kissed her cheek.

Charlotte started to respond but he was galloping downstairs.

'I'll start dinner.'

Charlotte stroked the dreamy, geometric lines of the box. It felt soothing. The pattern was stylish, flirty. Who has owned you, she wondered. On whose dressing-table have you sat?

'Look what I found today.'

Charlotte found Ben in the kitchen draining pasta.

'Where did you get that?'

'The new charity shop at Fryern Arcade.' Ben looked puzzled. 'You know, where the bakery was?'

'I thought that was going to be an estate agent's?'

'It's a charity shop now.'

'Well, this is Chandler's Ford. If it's not one, it's the other. I'm pleased you treated yourself to something, darling.'

'It was only £5. I hope you don't mind? I can walk to work a couple of days this week. Save the bus fare.'

Ben groaned. He placed the colander into the sink.

'Charlotte, I'm sorry it's like this. I keep hoping things will get better.'

He clasped her hands in his. His warm brown eyes searched her face.

'It's just that I want a baby so much, Ben.'

'We'll try next year. Come what may.'

'You've said that for the past 3 years. I'm 34 now.' Tears stung her eyes.

He looked crestfallen. 'It will happen. '

He enveloped her in a hug. Charlotte sank into him. His warm familiarity was comforting.

'I know I should be grateful. I've got you, our home, health. It's just…' She nestled further into his arms.

'It will work out, I promise.'

Later that evening, Ben worked on his laptop, preparing an urgent business forecast. Charlotte sat with the box in her lap, her fingers tracing the pattern. She heard a click. The top slid back. She gasped. Inside, underneath a layer of dust, was a brooch. Diamond-shaped, its peach and golden hues echoed the colours of the box. Fumbling with the old-fashioned clasp, she fixed it to her dark blouse. It sparkled like a radiant sunburst.

'Wow, look what I've found! Isn't it beautiful?'

Ben squinted at it.

'Looks like something from an old movie. Is it amber?'

'Coloured glass, I think.' Charlotte brushed her hand across the brooch. Startled, she held her palm out to Ben. 'It feels warm.'

'It's a striking piece. Wonder if it's worth anything?'

She heard fast tip-tapping as Ben keyed the laptop.

'Whoa, have a look at this.'

On the screen was a dazzling variety of Art Deco style brooches.

'That's the same as this one!' An identical brooch shimmered at the heart of the collection. 'Mine must be a copy.'

The next morning after an exchange of emails and calls with a London dealer, Charlotte was filled with gleeful astonishment.

'It's not a copy. It's an original.' She grasped Ben's hands.

'So the brooch is worth a fortune, but the box is more or less worthless?'

'It's the box I really like so I don't mind selling the brooch. I'm going to give a lot of the money to the charity shop.'

'Of course you must, love, there'll be enough of it to go around.'

As Charlotte got off the bus at the Fryern Arcade, she hummed. She felt so much happier today. The traffic queued as the crossing light turned green. She must thank the shop assistant. If she hadn't pushed Charlotte to buy at a knock-down price, their lives could never have changed like this.

A shaft of sunlight pierced the afternoon sky. The shop windows looked as dusty as before. She peered inside, noticing that the nautical mannequins had disappeared. Perhaps they were having a change of theme. Looking closer, she saw the interior was empty, except for squashed cardboard boxes, pieces of wood, and junk mail.

Puzzled, she read the sign pinned to the locked door:

"Coming next week, a brand new estate agency for Chandler's Ford."

Trembling, she felt for the brooch. Still there, nestling in her bag. She assumed the box was safe at home on her dressing table.

Charlotte wrinkled her nose. A waft of Youth Dew drifted past. She caught a glimpse of a middle-aged woman wearing cats-eye glasses turning the corner.

'Wait!'

It was the assistant, she was sure of it. By the time a lorry lumbered by, the assistant had disappeared. Charlotte shivered. Whatever would she tell Ben?

The Chalvington Road Coven

Catherine Griffin

Pam wasn't sure what to expect of a witch's house. Her only ideas involved gingerbread, which seemed unlikely. In fact, it was a large white bungalow on Chalvington Road.

Inside... There were some cobwebs and dust. Also a 1980's pine kitchen boasting an assortment of sickly house plants suspended in macramé pot-hangers. Newspapers and junk mail were piled on every surface except the round kitchen table. Blue flame from the gas burner licked up the side of a pressure cooker steaming on the hob.

Whatever was cooking smelt like rubbish left too long in the heat.

'Just boiling up some leftovers for soup.' Kelly gestured at the pan. Her hands were small and thin and crooked like a bird's claw. 'Why don't you sit down? Coffee? Tea?'

As Pam pulled out a chair, something soft brushed her leg.

'Oh, Sooty, there you are.' The older woman bent to stroke the cat as it wove around her.

Pam shut her eyes. Of course, she should have expected a cat. A black cat, what else?

'Are you all right?' Kelly said.

'Fine.' Pam took a deep breath and sat down. 'Cats make me nervous. It's silly, I know. One scratched me when I was a toddler.'

Kelly nodded, her head on one side. 'I understand. It's beards, with me. And avocados. Can't abide them. Anyway, just say if she's bothering you, and I'll throw her out.'

'No, it's fine. I should try and get used to them.'

A knock at the front door interrupted Kelly as she filled the kettle. 'That'll be Echo, I expect.'

The new arrival was young, much younger than the kitchen cabinets, Pam thought. Pretty too, if she hadn't been loaded with black make-up. As it was, the combination of long red hair and black lipstick was certainly striking. But if you've been saddled with a name like Echo, perhaps you have to look like that.

The girl stood in the doorway, frowning. 'Is this all of us?'

Her direct gaze made Pam uncomfortably aware of her own generous curves and clothes chosen for comfort. Kelly dressed from the charity shop, but even so, she had a certain style. She looked the part. Pam didn't. She never wore black, anyway; it made her look like a stack of tyres.

'Three is enough to start with,' Kelly said. 'If they're the right three.' She sat down at the table, and the other two joined her.

The older woman drew herself up very straight. 'Before we start, do we all agree that whatever we do here is just between us?'

Echo nodded. 'Secret.'

'I told my boys I joined a book group.' Butterflies fluttered

78

through Pam's stomach. 'We're reading The Kite Runner.'

'You understand we aren't doing anything wrong, but sometimes people can be very ignorant.'

Echo leaned forwards, black fingernails tapping the table. 'So what are we going to do?'

'I dabbled a little when I was younger,' Kelly said. 'But that was a long time ago. I thought we'd better start with a simple Invocation of Power. It's just a general ritual to raise positive spiritual energy.'

Echo looked disappointed. 'I thought we'd be doing real magic. Not silly healing-power-of-crystals New Age stuff.'

Kelly frowned. 'There's nothing silly about it. Now, did you bring the items I asked for?'

Pam reached for her carrier bag. 'I made a carrot cake, too.'

Echo spilled a handful of candles on the table. The long white tapers rolled towards Kelly. 'I can get a chicken, if you want.'

'Did we need a chicken? They're on special offer in Asda, I could have picked one up.' Pam put her cake tin on the table, together with the incense sticks.

'I mean a live one.' Echo rolled her eyes. 'I know someone keeps chickens.'

'What?' Pam stared at the young woman.

'Absolutely not,' Kelly said. 'The modern practice doesn't require cruelty to animals.'

'Oh, good. No eye of newt, then?' Pam giggled.

'I was just saying.' Echo picked up her candles. 'Because I could totally kill a chicken, if I had to.'

'Well, you won't need to. Now, can you draw a circle with the chalk?'

'On the table?' Echo fingered the dusty stub of white chalk.

'And a pentagram inside?'

'Yes, that's the idea. Pam, why don't you help me with the candles?'

'I don't see anything wrong with killing a chicken, really. I mean, if you buy one from Asda, someone killed it.' Echo completed her circle and stepped back to admire it.

'No chickens,' Kelly said. 'I'm vegetarian.'

'Oh. Fair enough. Is that OK?'

On the inscribed table, five candles burned at the points of the star, surrounding a small copper bowl in the centre. To Pam, it didn't look especially mystical, but Kelly seemed satisfied.

'Sit, and we'll begin.'

Kelly lit an incense stick and dropped it into the bowl. Smoke curled upwards and the cloying scent of sandalwood joined the steam from the pressure cooker. She closed her eyes.

'Now, just clear your minds and breathe for a moment. Meditate.'

Pam obediently closed her eyes and tried to think of nothing, but things kept intruding. Her shopping list, the laundry, new shoes for the boys... As soon as she pushed one away, a fresh worry popped up. What was she doing here? She'd just thought it would be nice to get out of the house and meet some new people. Have a hobby, like everyone else at work with their book groups and cycle rides and darts tournaments. Was it too much to ask, to have something for herself alone?

Something beeped.

'Oh, sorry. That's my phone.' Echo fumbled with her bag.

Kelly sighed. 'Please turn it off.'

'Right, right. It's just a text from my boyfriend.' Echo fiddled with the phone for a moment, then dropped it back in her bag. 'Sorry. It's off now.'

'Let's try again. If you're both quite ready... Just clear your mind. Think about what you desire. The thing you want more than anything in the world. Focus on that.'

Pam closed her eyes. What did she want? She had no idea. She knew what the boys wanted. They never stopped asking for things, most of which she couldn't afford.

'What I want is to be taken seriously,' Echo said. 'No one at work listens to me. I may be good looking, but that doesn't mean I don't have a brain.'

It might help if you wore less black eye-liner and smaller earrings, Pam thought. Ones without skulls and daggers. She sighed. Youth was wasted on the young.

'Does this work? Have you ever got what you wanted, Kelly?' Echo said.

'I haven't picked the winning lottery numbers yet, no. But there's always hope. A small windfall would do... enough for a new kitchen, say.'

Money, yes, I want money, Pam thought. But the idea didn't really excite her. Money would help, sure, but would it make her any happier than she was already? Life wasn't bad. She had two lovely sons, a home, a job she enjoyed. Everything she really needed.

The only thing she wanted was a little excitement. To be swept off her feet by a gorgeous strapping young man, possibly in uniform, that would be good. Not likely to happen, but if you're going to dream, you may as well dream the impossible. A smile spread across her face, accompanied by a sense of peace and calm certainty.

Something soft brushed against her ankle.

'Aaargh!' She jumped to her feet.

The table lurched; somehow, she'd gotten tangled with the table leg. Echo and Kelly grabbed the table as burning candles tumbled and rolled. The cat dashed out and leapt onto the kitchen worktop.

'Sorry.' Pam collapsed into her seat, her heart racing. 'The cat made me jump.'

Kelly frowned at the offending animal. 'Sooty, get off there. You know you aren't allowed.'

Sooty hopped over a pile of mail, knocking a roll of kitchen towel onto the cooker. A minor avalanche of paper slid to the floor.

'Oh, now look what you've done.' Kelly levered herself to her feet. 'Dang cat.'

Sensing it was in trouble, the cat jumped down and trotted out of the room, tail held high. Kelly huffed in annoyance.

'That didn't go so well.' The older woman scowled at the mess, then shook herself. 'Never mind. How about some tea, and we'll try that carrot cake?'

'Kelly...' Pam got to her feet. 'I'm so sorry, I...'

Echo screamed and pointed past Kelly, at the cooker. Flames licked up the side of the saucepan, consuming the kitchen roll.

'Fire!'

Some hours later, the three women sat in a row on the low wall in front of the house. Pam had a blanket round her shoulders. She wasn't sure why, as she was uncomfortably warm, but clutched it anyway.

'I'm so sorry,' she said. She'd already apologised several times, but it didn't seem enough.

Kelly patted her shoulder. 'No one's hurt, and there's no great damage done. The kitchen's ruined, I suppose. But I've got insurance. And you were so brave, rushing back in there to find Sooty.'

'Stupid, more like.' She hadn't felt brave when that fireman had dragged her out, though he'd been very nice about it. Of course, the cat was fine. Cats are always fine.

'You are brave,' Echo said. She rubbed her black-streaked face. 'I just panicked. You were so calm...'

'I didn't do anything special.' Looking back on it, she wondered why she hadn't been more scared. Time had seemed to slow, and she'd just done the logical things. Apart from looking for the cat, anyway.

The firemen were still going in and out of the house and tidying up their hoses. Her rescuer winked at Pam as he passed. She smiled back.

Echo looked at her phone. 'Gawd, look at the time. I have to go. I don't know what I'll tell my boyfriend, I must look a fright.'

Pam passed her a clean tissue. 'You know, you're a very pretty girl. You'd look nicer without all that black make-up.'

'Really?' Echo paused. 'It was nice meeting you today. I really enjoyed it, up until the fire. Shall we try again next month?'

Pam glanced at Kelly. 'Hmm. We could meet at my place... but I'm not sure about the whole witch thing. Maybe we should try something different. Less flammable. Like a book group?'

New Beginnings

Maggie Farran

Mark knew he was thinking like a jealous toddler. He couldn't help himself. His gorgeous wife, Chloe, appeared to love the baby more than him.

'Shall I pick Joe up?' he said when the baby started to cry.

'I'll do it myself. You can't breastfeed. There isn't a lot you can do to pacify him. You could cook the dinner. That would help me most.'

Mark knew he wasn't a great cook, but he did his best. He served up his version of spag bol. It tasted alright to him, but Chloe ate hers with one hand while she jiggled the baby up and down with the other.

He innocently asked her if she'd enjoyed the meal.

She snapped back, 'Do I look like I've enjoyed it? It's not an easy meal to eat with one hand.'

He stacked the dishwasher in a temper, crashing the plates down into the rack. He couldn't seem to do anything right since Joe had been born. He felt neglected and relegated to second place. Whenever baby Joe cried, she rushed to pick him up and cuddle him. She seemed to spend her entire time feeding, changing, or rocking him. Any offers of help from him had been ignored.

'Do you have to make such a noise with those dishes? Joe is asleep at last. You're going to wake him up if you're not careful,' Chloe said in a stage whisper.

Mark tiptoed over to the Moses basket where his tiny son was soundly asleep. He looked down at him and felt that surge of protective love that he had felt just after Joe had been born. He had felt like a strong knight then, who would fight anything or anyone to protect his son. It had been a wonderful feeling. He had imagined how it would be when he took his precious family home from Winchester hospital.

It had been nothing like that. The last few weeks had been a nightmare. Joe cried all the time. Chloe was exhausted and bad-tempered. She didn't seem to like him any more let alone love him. She didn't seem to want a knight to protect her and the baby, just a servant to cook and clean.

'My Mum brought the Christening cake round. She made it herself. It must have taken her hours to do all that icing. It's in the larder. Have a look. I'm off to bed now while Joe's asleep.'

Mark looked at the cake. It looked delicious. His mother-in-law always baked a tasty fruit cake. The icing was a shiny white and 'JOE' was piped in pale blue. There was a small teddy bear made out of blue icing with a red bow sitting smugly on top of the cake. He poured himself a large glass of red wine. He was so tempted to cut himself a large slice of the cake to go with it. Instead he broke off a small piece of the teddy's right arm. It tasted sickly sweet.

'Grow up, Mark,' he told himself. 'You're a proper grown-up now with responsibilities.' He drained his glass and poured himself another one. Family life was not quite the fairy tale he had imagined. He staggered up to bed before he was tempted to finish the bottle.

He awoke in the morning to the sound of Chloe sobbing beside him. He rolled over and then he thought better of it. He reached over to his wife and gently touched her shoulder.

'What's the matter love? Why are you crying?'

Chloe sat up and pushed his hand away. 'I'm crying because I've got so much to do. The Christening is this afternoon. I've got so much left to do. I can't cope. I'm exhausted'

'I'll help you. Just tell me what you want me to do.'

'There's nothing you can do to help. I might as well do it myself. It's no help if I have to explain every little thing to you.' She shouted.

Mark pulled on his clothes and stormed out of the house. He had never felt so useless. He walked until he started to calm down. He found himself at Waitrose and bought himself a strong black coffee. He sat down and tried to read the paper, but the words meant nothing to him. He was startled when someone joined him at his table.

'Hello, Mark, mind if I join you? What are you doing here on a Sunday morning?'

It was Chloe's mother, Kate.

'Hi, yes that's fine. Sit down. I could do with someone to talk to.'

'What's the matter? Is it Chloe?'

'I don't know how to explain. You know how much I love her and the baby. I just can't seem to do anything right. Chloe doesn't seem to want me involved with the baby. I feel redundant.'

Kate went quiet for a minute. Then she surprised him by her words. 'Chloe likes to be in charge. She always has since she was a little girl. She's a perfectionist. She finds it almost impossible to ask for help. She does need you. You'll find a way to get through to her.'

Mark didn't know what to say. He gazed down at the table. He got up slowly and touched his mother-in-law's hand. 'Thanks, Kate. That Christening cake looks ace by the way.'

He looked through the buckets of flowers and chose a large bunch of cream roses. When he got home Chloe was having a cup of tea. Joe was peacefully asleep in his pram. She looked up and smiled.

'Sorry about earlier. I was way out of order. I'm just so tired at the moment.'

He kissed the top of her head and gave her the flowers. 'These are for you, love. You know I really want to help with little Joe. I want to make things easier for you. I just don't know how I can help. You'll have to spell it out to me a bit more.'

Chloe laughed. 'You can start by putting these beautiful flowers in water for me. Then you can take Joe for a long walk while I get the house tidy for this afternoon. I've got to make the sandwiches and set the table too.'

When Mark and Joe arrived home the house was transformed. The Christening cake stood in the middle of the table. On the top the teddy with the short right arm looked at him with a reproachful smile iced on his face. Everything was ready for Joe's big day. Mark lifted him carefully out of the pram.

'You feed him, love and then I'll get him dressed while you get yourself ready.'

Mark had a shower and put on his new suit. Then he took Joe from Chloe. He very carefully undressed him and changed his nappy, trying not to gag.

'That's better, Joe. You're nice and clean now.'

He put the silk Christening gown on Joe. It was a difficult trying to squeeze his arms through the tight little arm holes, but he managed it. He did up the fiddly pearl buttons on the back. He looked at Joe and laughed. 'You look fab, Joe. It's your special day and you won't remember a thing about it.'

Chloe came down, looking stunning in the coffee-coloured lace dress she'd bought especially for the Christening. Mark whistled.

'You look smashing, love. No-one would think you'd just had a baby.'

'My two men don't look too bad either.'

Chloe grinned. They set off for Saint Edward's church together. Mark pushed the pram with their precious son sleeping peacefully inside.

Zombie Experience, Part 2

Sally Howard

Sean woke with a start, gripping the edge of the makeshift cot in the cupboard that passed for a medical room. He lay for a minute, counting his breathing and staring at the damp-spotted ceiling.

What had happened?

A memory tugged at the back of his mind. He'd had a goddamn awful headache. He could remember that much.

He swung his legs over the side of the cot, dropped them to the cool linoleum, and staggered over to the sink in the corner. Oh god, what a sight stared back at him from the mirror. Pasty with undertones of swamp-green. Must be the strip light overhead, flickering and buzzing like a dying insect. He rubbed at his bloodshot eyes.

He remembered. A guest, yes, a lady, in his room. A white fleshy shoulder. He pushed at his temple trying to squeeze out the jumble of images. A blue-veined arm. He'd sniffed her arm.

The door clicked open behind him. Frank, their team

leader, stood with ever-present clipboard in hand, looking him up and down.

'Good, you're up. Hope you're feeling better. We're short tonight and I can't afford for you to miss your shift.'

'What happened?'

'It's pretty hot in there. Guess you fainted, mate.'

Sean straightened up, wiping his forehead and straightening his old t-shirt. He'd taken such pains to rip and roll this t-shirt in mud for this, his dream job.

'Nothing else?' he said.

Frank shrugged. 'Guys found you collapsed in a corner. Brought you in here.' He slapped him on the shoulder. 'Drink plenty of water and you'll be fine. 20 minutes, OK?'

Frank retreated out the door, seemingly satisfied with Sean's acquiescence. Sean scrunched up the paper towel and tossed it in the bin. Something felt very wrong. He knew it, without defining exactly what it was. Darned if he was going out there again.

Then he remembered Amelie.

His shoulders were rigid with expectation as he scanned the frosty images on the screens, waiting for the starter siren for the evening shift. Please don't let Amelie have come.

'Looking for someone?' Carl appeared beside him, white-faced and beer-breathed. Sean ignored him and continued to scan the screens. He thought he saw Amelie's auburn hair in a side room, but couldn't be sure.

'Looking for another tasty arm?' said Carl.

The image of white flesh flashed in front of his eyes. His

stomach curdled at the thought. He turned to Carl, who was licking his lips. He winced. Grotesquely, Carl's tongue was heavily coated in white fur.

'What on earth are you talking about?' he stuttered.

'Whoever it is,' Carl slapped him on the back. 'Enjoy.'

What's with the back-slapping? He stood immobile as the starter siren blared and Carl disappeared through the doors. Dread forced its way into his stomach and settled in for the night. Something was not right about this place, not right big time. He squeezed his hands into fists. He needed to find Amelie. To get her out of here as soon as possible.

He ran down the main corridor, past party-going teenagers dressed in t-shirts and skinny jeans. He found Amelie at the far end, coming up behind her and encircling her slim wrist in his hand. She jumped and squeaked but he guided her into a side room.

She put her arms round his neck and pulled in for a cuddle. 'I thought I wasn't going to find you.'

The room was empty except for a half-collapsed metal bedstead, a hangover from when the building was a Victorian hospital. A fake oil lamp glowed on the red-painted walls. He headed towards the shadows at the opposite end. He looked down into her face, a faint sheen on her forehead, due to the closeness in the building. 'Where's Robyn?' he said, 'She was coming with you, yeah?'

'She went home. She didn't like it.'

'Are you sure?'

'Yes, I waited with her. Her dad came. They went back to Chandler's Ford.' A crease furrowed her forehead. He was always amazed by how round her eyes were. They widened even more now. 'Why? What's the matter?' she said.

'It's not safe here. We need to leave.'

'What do you mean? You're scaring me.'

'There's something going on. I don't know what. But we need to leave.' He tucked her head under his chin where it fitted so perfectly. He'd got her into this. He'd get her out.

They stood for a moment listening to the sounds of players in other rooms. There was a high-pitched squeal then sounds of girls laughing. Guess they were OK for a while. He buried his nose in Amelie's hair. It smelt so fresh, cherry blossom on a spring day. She was wearing her Walking Dead t-shirt. Slightly too big, it fell off one shoulder. He bent his head. She smelt so good tonight. He sniffed deeply, pushing his nose onto her silky skin, opening his mouth ...

Dread kicked him in the stomach. What on earth was he doing? He pushed her away.

'What was that for?' She stared at him, screwing together her eyebrows. A flush spread over her cheeks.

'Sorry, I didn't mean that.' She scrutinised his face and he had to lower his eyes. 'We've got to go, that's all.' His words came out too fast.

She continued to look at him askance. He didn't know himself, let alone be able to explain what was going on to her. She spun on her heel and made towards the door. 'Which way then?' she said, putting her hand on her hips.

Sean felt the edge of a headache returning, but now was not the time to think about that. He just needed to get out of this place, get some fresh air and distance to be able to get a perspective on things. An exit sign glowed a dull green over a door half way down the corridor. He pushed the emergency exit handle and started down the dimly lit steps. Amelie clattered down behind him.

Half way down the stairs split into two, a staircase descending to the right and left. No indication which was the exit. Right was a good a direction as any. He started down the next flight, Amelie keeping pace with him now, but continuing to say nothing.

They reached the bottom of the stairs and were confronted by a door secured with a key lock.

'Look.' Amelie pointed to a faded notice taped to the wall. Leaning forward to see in the low light, Sean read out: 'From now on, the key code will be changed every month. Speak to Maeve.'

'Maeve? Your sister? She's in charge of security?'

He shrugged. 'Dunno. She's never been, like, security minded. She uses 1234 on her iPad. '

'Well, try that.'

His fingers slid off the small shiny grey buttons and he fumbled the first attempt at entering Maeve's code. Amelie gently pushed him away and pressed the straightforward key code. To his amazement, the handle yielded, the heavy door swinging open softly on well-oiled hinges. So much for Maeve's approach to security.

Sean stuck his head in. In contrast to the rest of the disused building, this was a well-lit room with freshly painted white walls and clean grey tiles on the floor. Along one wall ran a workbench, with a sink, metal implements, and a couple of microscopes. A glass cabinet held a row of labelled bottles and vials containing an amber liquid of seemingly varying strengths. White lab coats were piled up on a hook at the end. Above the computer and a stack of CDs, a poster of the periodic table hung askew from dried-up blu-tack. On the other side of the room, there appeared to be cages along the wall, about 6 feet high, covered in grey tarpaulin.

Sean and Amelie edged into the room. Sean clicked the door shut behind them. He had an uneasy feeling that they had come to a dead end. A wooden door at the other end was half open. He could see a broom and plastic mop in a metal bucket in the closet beyond. A polished steel door next to the cupboard looked like a freezer. They should've taken the other fork in the stairs. It was sure to have led to the exit. He cursed gently under his breath. He heard a faint shuffling sound from under the tarpaulins.

'Stinks in here,' said Amelie, wrinkling her nose. 'Bad drains.'

Sean moved to the steel door and tried the handle. Locked solid. He rattled it in frustration.

A noise, like a moan, came from behind the tarpaulins accompanied by further shuffling. He met Amelie's eyes.

'What was that?' she mouthed.

Amelie approached the tarpaulin and put her hand on it.

'I wouldn't do that if I were you.'

They whipped round to see Carl standing in the doorway. In the bright overhead light, he looked more wasted than ever, greasy make-up running in streaks down his wan face. He closed the door and stood in front of it with his arms crossed over his chest. He blinked his bloodshot eyes rapidly. Sean pulled Amelie back, glancing towards the rear of the room.

'Sean, Sean,' he said, in a raspy voice. 'Are you leaving? I thought better of you. I thought you were going to join me.'

'Join you? What are you talking about?'

96

'Got a headache coming on again, have you?'

Sean swallowed hard. Carl was not making any sense. Join him with what? And headache? Yes, it was true, he couldn't shift this hangover. Then realisation swept over him like an arctic blast. They'd given him something, hadn't they?

'What have you done?' he shouted. More rustling under the tarpaulins.

'I thought you were the kinda guy who enjoyed a good time. Who wasn't averse to trying something new.'

Carl approached the glass cabinet, took a key out of his ratty jeans pocket and inserted it into the cabinet lock. Reaching in, he took out a small glass vial. Holding his thumb over the cork stopper, he gave it a little shake.

'This formula,' he said, 'You want it.'

'Why would I want that?'

'I gave you a massive dose.'

'What? What is it? Are you trying to poison me?'

'Poison, oh, no, no. It's not poison.' He chuckled. 'This,' he said, holding it to his nose, drawing in a deep sniff, 'is my own special batch. For you, I modified it slightly, made it stronger. I wanted to see the effects, how much you could handle.'

'Why would you do that? You're mad!'

'Yeah, crazy, mad scientist. I'm practising the laugh.'

Amelie had remained silent, but now stepped to look into Carl's face. 'What have you done to him?'

'Don't worry, darling, he's alright. He's just developed a little appetite for flesh.'

'Oh my god, what have you done?'

Fire coursed through his blood. He rushed at Carl. He was going to smash his head in.

97

He didn't see the punch coming. It hit him hard under the ribs, the force reverberating through his internal organs. He fell to his knees. Another punch followed, like being hit with a baseball bat, pushing air out of his lungs in a grunt. Carl kicked him sideways and his head hit the tiles with a crunch. His vision tunnelled.

Tarpaulin cracked as it was scraped to the floor. A bolt rang as it was drawn back. A cage door squeaked on its hinges. Sean heard steps as Carl ran to the door. The door clicked shut. A bolt shot fast on the other side

Amelie was at his side. 'Sean, Sean, are you alright?' she shouted. 'Get up. Get up.'

Face still pressed to the cold tile, Sean could see the feet of someone shuffling towards them. He pulled his head up to see a grey-suited businessman walking with the jerky movements of someone lacking control of his limbs. The man was masticating like he was chewing gum. Behind him, he saw two more figures.

Jolted into action, he pushed himself up, legs trembling. He felt like he'd been kicked by a horse. Probably a cracked rib.

Amelie grabbed the stack of CDs and cradled them in her arms. She drew her lips back in a snarl. She flicked a CD like a Frisbee. It sliced into the eye of a slack-jawed woman that was coming at her, slicing through her eye like a hot knife through an egg. Blood splattered over Amelie. She didn't seem to notice.

The woman kept coming on and Amelie readied the next CD. Sean grabbed a tray of glass flasks from the bench and threw it. It bounced off the grey suit of the businessman and smashed on the floor. What a lame throw!

He desperately searched for another weapon. Seeing the mop in the closet, he grabbed it. He brandished it in front of him.

Dammit, he thought, a mop! Shaking the stringy head like a puppet, he managed to distract the people, if that's what they were (a woman and an overweight boy) from Amelie. As they turned towards him, shuffling, groaning, grinding their teeth, he turned the mop head round. He hesitated. This was the moment of truth. Putting all his weight behind it, he shoved the end of the plastic mop at the teenager. It glanced off his cheek, useless.

This wasn't how it was in the movies, where the hero dispatches the hordes of undead without breaking a sweat. What was he talking about? The undead? He almost laughed. He was drenched. Sweat was trickling into his eyes. He could hardly see.

He took a steadying breath. The putrid smell in the room was gag-worthy. It must be coming from the people. Now he looked more closely, he saw that their skin was grey-tinged, elephant-like. They had the staring eyes of the red-eye flight.

Gripping the only weapon he had, he shoved again. The handle hit its target. Shoving upwards, he felt it crunch into chin bone. He felt sick, hot, cold all over. Relief spread through him as the person – thing - slumped to the floor.

Amelie turned to him, eyes wide with fear. She was running out of CDs to throw. He backed up until the bench dug into his back. Amelie's foot clunked against the silver door. She turned, ran her hands over the metal door searching for a handle. She thumped her fists, shouting for help, her voice high-pitched, panicky. They were cornered.

Suddenly the door cracked open. A hand pulled her through. Sean punched the mop handle at the chest of a zombie and ran for the door.

'Maeve?'

Sean stumbled, half fell into the room. It was all quite normal. A windowless office with a utility brown desk and silver MacBook lying closed on it. A grey filing cabinet stood in the corner, next to a hat stand with coats on it.

Standing in front of the desk was his older sister, Maeve. Maeve, never seen in anything other than faded ripped jeans and slouchy t-shirt, even on the smartest of family occasions, was attired in a modest grey trouser suit, crisp white shirt and kitten heels. He gawped. Somehow this picture of professionalism was more baffling than the events that had unfolded in the lab next door.

'Maeve,' he repeated.

At the other end of the room, lounging in chairs with their feet up on another desk, were Bevvie and Jimbo.

A frown creased Maeve's forehead. 'Sean, are you OK? I was worried when we lost you. And, Amelie too, I'm so sorry about this. I'm afraid we didn't know you were coming tonight.'

Sean tried to pull together the fragments floating in his brain. 'What on earth is going on? Who were those people? Why did they attack us? How are they like that?'

'Who, what, why, how. Yes, lots of questions. I'll try and answer them, but take a seat first. And Bevvie and Jimbo, perhaps a cup of tea?'

Sean continued to stand like a dumb-founded dog. Maeve pulled out a chair and indicated for him to sit. They both flopped into chairs to the soothing, normal, sound of a kettle coming to the boil and the clink of mugs.

Maeve perched on the edge of her desk. 'Nano technology and disease,' she said. 'Both highly lucrative in their own right. And now brought together. ProNano industries, a conglomerate of

100

healthcare and IT companies, invented microscopic nanobots, which can be injected into the bloodstream, latch onto diseased cells and destroy them. All good so far.

'However, in 2012, disgruntled employee Bob Carson, apparently, left a little time bomb in response to, what he considered, being unfairly fired.'

Bevvie and Jimbo handed round mugs of tea. Amelie cupped it in her hands, the steam rising to curl her hair round her face.

'So what did he do?' asked Amelie.

'He made the nanobots self-replicate, which means they want to transfer from host to host, which they do by biting a hole in a healthy victim and streaming in to take up residence. No one has been able to de-activate it.'

'What about this Bob Carson guy? Can't you find him?' asked Sean.

'Tried, can't find him.' Maeve sighed. 'The real beauty is that the nanobots keep changing. As soon as you think you've got them, they disappear and then re-appear elsewhere with a different format.'

'What happens to people who are infected?'

'Gets into your brain. Takes over.' Bevvie twisted her finger against her temple, like she was drilling into her brain.

'That's revolting.' Amelie put down her tea, and hugged herself. 'How many are infected?'

'We're not sure. Possibly hundreds.'

'What? Wandering around outside? I don't believe it. Not for one second. It'd be all over the news.' Sean glared at his sister. This was all utterly ridiculous.

At a glance from his sister, Bevvie reached for the remote

on the table and flicked on a TV attached the wall. She pressed play on the DVD.

'This is what we've seen so far. Remember this? Fire fighters called to a burning warehouse on an Eastleigh industrial estate? It was in the news.'

'Uh-huh.' He nodded. Images of a factory lit up by flames against a night sky.

'People were advised to keep their windows and doors closed to stop toxic fumes getting into their homes. Only, there weren't any toxic fumes.'

Sean shook his head. 'You've got to be kidding me.'

'It's real. Slow spreading, as yet. Contained but covered up.'

He rubbed his hand over the back of his neck. He tried to factor this new reality. Reanimation? In England, Hampshire? He chuckled. Not really cricket, was it?

'I'm sorry. I was just thinking. I mean, it's ludicrous.'

'Sit for a while, you look exhausted,' said Maeve. 'And you'll need time to digest the information. 'Scuse the pun.' She nodded to Bevvie and Jimbo. 'In the meantime we've got some cleaning up to do.'

Bevvie and Jimbo went to a grey metal cabinet in the corner of the room. Jimbo unlocked the padlock and swung the door open to reveal a row of long stiletto knives like bayonets for mounting on the end of a rifle. Jimbo and Bevvie picked up one each. Bevvie used the polished reflection in the blade to quickly pin back her hair. They returned to the door that Sean and Amelie had come through and disappeared.

'Regrettable loss,' said his sister.

'What? To get rid of those flesh-eating...'

'Zombies? Is that the word you're looking for?' A smile flitted over her lips.

Amelie slumped down in her chair. Sean put his arm round her shoulder. Tiredness bent her shoulders. She leaned forward, hugging her knees.

Maeve passed her a paper towel. She nodded at the black, dirty streaks down her bare arm. Wrinkling her nose, Amelie jabbed at the mess with the towel.

'Nice fighting out there, by the way, both of you.'

'I guess we didn't have a choice.'

They sat in silence for a while. A clock on the wall ticked loudly. 11:45pm. Sean's shoulders sagged with weariness. What a day.

No sounds came from the other side of the door. Maeve was leafing through a sheaf of papers. She seemed unconcerned. Guess Bevvie and Jimbo could look after themselves.

The metal door swung open and Bevvie and Jimbo slipped back into the room. Bevvie's cheeks glowed but other than small tendril of black hair escaping from her braid, she hadn't broken a sweat. She smiled. 'All sorted.'

A bubble formed at the back of Sean's throat. Just another day at the office. He felt an irresistible urge to laugh at all of this craziness. No one else seemed to be the slightest bit fazed. He looked over at Amelie. She shrugged her shoulders, equally nonplussed.

'Any sign of Carl?' asked Maeve.

'No. Looks like he's taken a batch of vaccine and the formula bottle,' said Bevvie.

'We'll have to deal with him.'

'He said I'd had some formula?' said Sean. 'What did he

103

mean?'

'We think he spiked your drink. Normally we administer the vaccine, or formula as he called it, under controlled conditions. It has, er, certain side-effects.'

'Like what?'

'It turns you into a zombie for 24 hours,' said Bevvie. Emitting a low moan, she crossed her eyes and started to shuffle round the room.

'Thank you, Bevvie. We take a small amount of a re-programmed nanobot serum. Quite simply, if you were bitten, the infection would think that the host was already infected and become non-active. It provides a measure of protection.'

'But no protection if one of those critters tries to chomp your leg off,' said Jimbo. Bevvie bumped into him and pretended to chew his arm.

'And we can't vaccinate on a wider scale because we'd have a load of flesh-eaters wandering around for at least a short period of time.' Bevvie released Jimbo's arm and blew him a kiss.

'Jerome and Maddie are working on the problem. They're our PHD students up at Oxford.'

'Why did he give it to me? He said he'd altered it, made it stronger.'

'Like he was testing it, maybe, to see how addictive it was,' said Maeve. 'What else did he say?'

'He wanted me to join him. I've no idea why. I've hardly ever spoken to him.'

'Perhaps he was just picking on the new guy. It does make me wonder what he intends.'

'Wants to be leader of his own little gang.' Bevvie snorted. 'Always was full of himself.'

'Makes sense,' said Maeve, 'We need to find him.'

Maeve turned to Sean. 'I'm sorry. It looks like he gave you a major dose. How much, I don't know, and maybe because you were drunk it dissipated the effects. But sufficient that there was no way you could have stopped yourself from doing what you did.'

'Doing what I did? And what was that? Did I ... erm? Just tell me what happened, OK?'

Maeve dropped her eyes.

A cold wave, rising from the ocean's dark depths, swept over him, confronting him with a possible truth. Had he killed someone, taken a life, another human, a woman who'd thought she was here for an afternoon's entertainment?

'What happened to her?' The words choked in his throat, but he needed to know, whatever the outcome.

'We tried the vaccine, but it was too late.'

He ground his jaw. He fisted his hands. He was disgusted with himself. He was no better than those biting blood-suckers next door. He was a detestable monster. An abomination. He needed to be put down. He ...

Amelie reached up and touched his jawline. He turned away. How could she possibly want to stay with him now? How could he stay with her, knowing what he was? His heart shrivelled inside at the necessity of losing her.

Her hand was on his cheek, turning his head, reaching her hands round the nape of his neck. He looked down into her blue-green eyes, wide, open windows to her heart. The desire to be comforted, to kiss and comfort in return, was overwhelming, a tornado sweeping away all resolve.

Maeve gave them a moment. 'There's something else,' she said. 'Depending on how much he gave you, you may find it addictive. The serum is the nanobot technology. We give enough to provide protection, but not enough to give you the desire to eat flesh. Well, normally not enough.'

'You mean, I'm going to want to keep on biting people?'

'Possibly.'

'Oh great. And how bad is this going to be? Am I gonna be able to I trust myself?' He looked at Amelie.

'It depends. Have you felt anything, any desire to eat, er, flesh?'

Oh god, he groaned.

'But Carl wasn't attacking us like the zombies, was he?' said Amelie. 'He didn't appear to want to eat our flesh. He was drinking the vaccine.'

'I suspect he's found a way of controlling it already. He's always been very much in control, which made him our best fighter.' She sighed, then stood up. 'Sean, Amelie, I'm sorry that you've become involved, but you have, and that's a fact that can't be changed. But you've proved your worth. You'd be invaluable to our cause. I'd like you to join us. Find Carl before he goes and does this to someone else.'

Sean knew his decision at once. He needed to put this right. He needed to put himself right. Then he could be with Amelie, properly, rightfully.

'I'm in, but keep Amelie out of it,' he said.

Amelie reached for his hand, interlocking her fingers. 'We're a team. Don't ever forget that. I'm not leaving you to fight this all by yourself.'

'It's dangerous. I can't let you be in danger.'

'It's my choice.'

'But ...'

'Yes,' said Amelie to Maeve, 'That's my decision.'

'So we're in,' Sean said, 'Signed up, bona fide zombie fighters. Who'd have thought, eh?'

Afterword

We hope you enjoyed reading this book. If you did, or even if you didn't, please take a moment to leave your honest review on Amazon. Whether it's one star or five, reviews help authors and other readers.

This book would not have been possible without the support and help of Barbara Large and our fellow Creative Writing students. If you are reading this, thank you!

Maggie Farran
Catherine Griffin
Sally Howard
Karen Stephen

Printed in Great Britain
by Amazon